*Rescue Me Saga*

# Reading Order

The books in this series are not stand-alone novels. Please read in order because in a saga, of course, characters recur to continue working on real-life problems in later books.

The first six full-length Rescue Me Saga titles are available in e-book and print formats, as is the first collection of "Extras":

*Masters at Arms & Nobody's Angel (Combined Volume)*

*Nobody's Hero*

*Nobody's Perfect*

*Somebody's Angel*

*Nobody's Lost*

*Nobody's Dream*

*Western Dreams (Rescue Me Saga Extras #1)*

Standalone:

*Roar*

kallypsomasters.com/books

Kallypso Masters has no intention of ending the Rescue Me Saga, but will be writing spin-off standalone books (like **Roar**) and series (including a romantic-suspense trilogy with three romances featuring Mistress V. Grant, Gunnar Larson, and Patrick Gallagher). As much as she loves engaging with her readers, Kally writes by inspiration and follows the demands of her characters, so she cannot write to deadlines or predict whose story will come next. So be sure to subscribe to her newsletter (kallypsomasters.com/newsletter) so you can be sure not to miss any release announcements!

*Ginger,*
*Saddle up and enjoy*
*the ride — again!*

# Western Dreams

## (Rescue Me Saga Extras #1)

### Secret Scenes featuring
### Ryder & Megan and
### Luke & Cassie

*Kallypso Masters*

## Kallypso Masters

Copyright © 2016
Ka-thunk Publishing

Western Dreams
(Rescue Me Saga Extras #1)
Kallypso Masters

Copyright © 2016
Ka-thunk! Publishing
Print Edition
E-book ISBN: 978-1941060247
Print ISBN: 978-1941060254

Original e-book version: August 2016
Original Print version: August 2016

Edited by Meredith Bowery and Ekatarina Sayanova
Cover design by Linda Lynn
Cover image licensed though DepositPhotos;
Image graphically altered by Linda Lynn
Formatted by BB eBooks

This book contains content that is NOT suitable for readers 17 and under.

To discover more about this book and others, see the *Other Books By Kallypso Masters* section at the end of this book. For more about Kallypso Masters, please go to the About the Author section.

# Dedication

To Mr. Ray, my hubby, who didn't think I could ever write something this short.

And to all my loyal fans, I hope you'll enjoy this special visit with these members of the Rescue Me Saga family.

# Acknowledgements

This **Western Dreams** collection of Rescue Me Saga extras wouldn't have come about if I hadn't needed something to put in the welcome bags for KallypsoCon 2016: Western Romance. I decided to update readers on my two most "western" characters—Luke & Cassie and Ryder & Megan, whose lives were joined on Luke's ranch at the end of **Nobody's Dream** and will continue to be entwined in future books.

I want to thank my editors for this collection—Meredith Bowery, who always keeps an eye on my continuity issues with past books, and Ekatarina Sayanova, who corrects my grammar and provides BDSM expertise.

A special thanks to my author friend Tymber Dalton who allowed me to consult with her on the bullwhip scene to make sure it was safe, sane, and consensual.

My thanks to my awesome beta readers—Margie Dees, Iliana Gkioni, Kelly Mueller, Ruth Reid, and Lisa Simo-Kinzer—for saving me from embarrassing errors and to help me give other readers the best possible experience. Some of them even helped me figure out how to complete what was missing from one of the scenes.

As with anything I write—long or short—I rely on Facebook's The Rescue Me Saga Discussion Group for advice and feedback. Someone in the group (or perhaps several someones) suggested the title **Western Dreams** for this collection when I was stumped, but Facebook deleted the thread before I could note whom to acknowledge here. They know who they are, though. Thank you!

Thanks also to my last-minute proofreading crew who always find the things I miss (or new mistakes I make after the editors sign off on it). Namely, my proofreaders for **Western Dreams** are Annette Elens, Barb Jack, Alison Klinkhammer, Angelique Luzader, Eva Meyers, Christine Mulcair, and Lisa Simo-Kinzer. Ladies, as always you did an awesome job!

# Author's Note

Normally, when I finish an epic-length novel like **Roar** (released in June 2016), I take a month off to recover and refill the well before starting on a new writing project. But with KallypsoCon looming, Ryder and Luke would *not* leave me alone. The day after **Roar** released, I started to dabble with a few ideas for scenes that either hadn't been shared with you in **Nobody's Dream** or take place after that book ended.

If you're new to my books or haven't caught up with book six in the series, please note that this collection is not a standalone and is filled with spoilers from **Nobody's Dream** and earlier books in the Rescue Me Saga. I encourage you to read those first starting with the free-at-the-moment book one, **Masters at Arms & Nobody's Angel**. If you enjoy that one, please continue through the series and move to **Western Dreams** after **Nobody's Dream**.

These five stories poured out of me in about a month. It was refreshing to be able to revisit old friends who probably wouldn't have a sequel for years at the pace I write. In **Western Dreams**, I didn't bring up new problems or resolve any major conflicts from the previous books. I'll save those for when these couples come together in **Somebody's Dream** someday. Instead, this collection is filled with fun, sexy glimpses into the lives of these couples. The first two sections with Ryder & Megan are scenes that took place "off the page" in **Nobody's Dream**, followed by three other sections updating us on Ryder & Megan's and Luke & Cassie's journeys after that book ended.

Now, sit back, pour yourself a glass of wine (or Coors beer might be appropriate, as you'll see in the honeymoon story in the first section), and enjoy visiting with old friends. Oh, and you might want to be prepared to grab your partner or vibrator after you finish the collection—or perhaps after finishing each story—because there are some very hot scenes in this collection.

You're welcome!

Oh, and please don't skip over the ***Roar*** excerpt in the back. I chose an equally hot scene to match the vignettes in this collection and leave my readers satisfied without spoiling the read if they haven't had a chance to pick it up yet.

Enjoy!
*Kally*

# Ryder & Megan:
# The Honeymoon

Ryder Wilson rolled the throttle as he rode up the dusty mountain road, his bride's arms wrapped around his waist. He and Megan had set off on their honeymoon about a week after they'd married. Of course, they'd had no problem celebrating their newlywed status at home before that. Carlos's home, that is. But Megan wanted to see her brother and his new triplets, even though Ryder wasn't ready to face his former master sergeant given the fact he hadn't been informed of the marriage yet.

Planning to take his time making their way to Denver, from Albuquerque, they'd stopped briefly at the Four Corners and started to tour Mesa Verde when he'd come close to having a panic attack. Too many people around for his peace of mind. After noticing the mention of a Colorado mountain on a tourist's shirt, he'd consulted his map app and then a park ranger, who let him in on how to find this hidden gem to show Megan. It was right on the way to one of the stops he'd already planned to stop, the Black Canyon of the Gunnison.

After stopping for lunch at Cortez, they headed north until he found the gravel road he'd been told to watch for. The Road King growled as the climb grew steeper.

"How much farther?" Megan shouted in his ear.

"You'll know when the hog stops rumbling."

Her laugh made him hard. He hoped the mid-June night wouldn't be too cold for them to camp out. They had sleeping bags and a pup tent stowed in their gear, but even with the additional touring rack and deluxe saddlebags he'd added, his HD Road King had limited storage capacity. If they planned to do a lot of touring together, Megan might want to have her own Harley—maybe a Softail. But right now, he wanted the feel of her right behind him.

At last, the gravel parking area spread out before them. He looked around to see if there was a visitors' information sign to help him get his bearings. Would they be able to see the peak from the trail—and know it when they saw it?

After staking out one of the two remaining campsites, he helped Megan off the bike and secured their helmets and saddlebags. Treated water was available here so they filled their sports bottles and hit the head before setting out. They'd see the campsite enough tonight.

Ryder bent down to kiss Megan, parting her lips as he deepened it before pulling away and smiling. "I can't wait to share something special with you on our hike." His voice had grown husky from desire.

"Sounds like fun." She wiggled her eyebrows.

He shook his head. "You, my horny wife, have a one-track mind. That wasn't what I had in mind at all—not for the hike, anyway. Now I hope you won't be let down by the actual surprise."

She brushed her thumb over his cheek and gave him a peck on the lips. "You never disappoint me, Sir."

God, he hoped he never would, either. Grabbing Megan's hand, he led her to the Woods Lake trailhead. A horse whinnied nearby. This campsite provided a loop for those with horses, too.

"It's gorgeous here. How'd you ever locate it with all the twists and turns on those back roads?"

"I'm pretty good at remembering directions. And then there's GPS." He grinned at her.

"Well, one secret has been revealed at least."

*   *   *

Megan hadn't felt so carefree in years. They were in no hurry to arrive at Adam's, because she wanted to give him and Karla plenty of time to settle in with the triplets. Okay, maybe Megan wanted to postpone seeing Karla surrounded by three beautiful babies, because Megan wouldn't be able to have even one herself.

*But that was my choice.*

She'd only wanted to rid herself of the pain of endometriosis, but never expected to fall in love with Ryder or any other man. Would he regret their not being able to have his biological children? He said they would adopt, but the process could take years. Not that they were in any hurry. They'd only been married a little over a week. Selfishly, she wanted to be able to do things like this with him before being tied down.

He hadn't told her much about where they'd be going on this trip. After walking around the Four Corners Monument for bragging rights that their honeymoon had taken place in four states, though, she'd become aware that Ryder's nerves were on edge by the time they reached Mesa Verde. The next thing she knew, he'd found this hidden gem far from the crowds. Perfect.

"Let's stop and drink," Ryder suggested. "I hear the more water we drink the easier the altitude will be on us."

Taking a few gulps, she wondered what it was he wanted to show her up here, given he didn't seem to have been here before, either, but she chose to stay in the moment instead.

Glancing over the meadow strewn with alpine flowers in purples, whites, and yellows, the backdrop of high mountains still showed a substantial amount of snow. Setting down her water bottle, she lifted her camera out of her backpack. "I've got to take some photos."

"Absolutely. Go ahead. I'm sure they'll bring back lots of

memories in the years to come."

Megan smiled, picturing them decades from now, perhaps on an anniversary, poring over the photos and remembering their honeymoon. She walked closer to a clump of flowers and snapped close-ups, then stood to take a longer shot of the entire meadow. Aspens with their off-white trunks and quaking leaves framed the shot. "I wonder which peaks these are."

"No clue. But there's one farther along I think I'll recognize when I see it."

She returned to his side and slung her camera strap around her neck. "Lead on!"

The path worn between the field grasses was narrow, but they chose to walk side by side a while, holding hands. "It's so peaceful up here. Like we're the only people in the world."

He squeezed her hand. "Thanks for understanding back at Mesa Verde."

"Nothing to thank me for. I was feeling a bit claustrophobic myself. I can't wait to show you Bandelier when we go home. Similar cliff dwellings but much more remote." She wondered how he would do in Denver, but there was no getting around eventually showing up at Adam's. They had a baby shower planned for the twenty-fourth.

Plenty of days for her and Ryder to enjoy their honeymoon road trip.

Ryder stopped along the trail as if to get his bearings and glanced up at the peaks surrounding them. His face lit in a smile, and he turned his attention to her before pointing to one. "See that mountain?"

She followed the direction of his finger to a sheer rock face and a snowpack. It seemed oddly familiar, although she wasn't familiar with Colorado's Fourteeners at all, except for Mount Evans near Denver. "Gorgeous! Where have I seen it before?"

"Well, it's the mountain face used on the Coors beer label."

"Your favorite."

"Yeah, but that's not why this mountain is important to *us*." She met his gaze, curious how a mountain could have any significance for them other than being beautiful to look at. After a dramatic pause, he said, "That, my dear Mrs. Wilson, is Wilson Peak."

Seriously? How sweet was it that he'd hiked all the way up here to show her this hidden mountain bearing his name? Wait. Wilson was *her* name now, too. She smiled as she turned toward the peak again, this time feeling a connection that hadn't been there a moment before.

"Any relation?"

"To the mountain?" he asked, teasing her.

She lightly punched his bicep. "No, silly, I'm asking if you're any relation to whomever the peak was named for."

"No clue. I only learned there was a Fourteener named Mount Wilson from a T-shirt someone was wearing at Mesa Verde." Such an observant man, even when being bombarded by so many people, he would take notice of something like that. "Then I asked the park ranger there, and she told me about it but said not to confuse it with Wilson Peak. Both are in the same vicinity here in the San Juan Mountains, but hearing about the Coors connection made me think it would be worth searching out."

As she stared at the mountain, Ryder came up behind her and wrapped his arms around her. His hands roamed over her belly to reach inside her leather jacket and cup her breasts, and she wished she'd worn a tank without bra cups. Undeterred, though, he pinched her nipples through the cups and leaned forward to kiss her on the neck.

"Are you sure you want to start something you can't finish, Ryder?"

He whispered in her ear, "Who says I'm not going to finish?" His right hand drifted lower until he briefly rubbed her clit through her jeans. Megan ground her butt against his erection and moaned. While they were partially hidden by the trees here, they were still on a well-marked trail. What if someone else happened upon them?

The friction of his fingers and her clothing against her clit had her squirming. She glanced around, hoping to find a place where they might remove some of the interfering layers of clothing and relieve this tension.

"Mr. Wilson?" she whispered.

He pulled her lower body tighter against his as he continued to nibble at her neck. "Hmm?"

"Before we reach *our* peak, do you think we ought to seek out a more secluded spot for this quickie?"

His left hand pinched her nipple, which only fueled the fire inside. "Who said anything about me taking you quickly? My bride, I can see you have a lot to learn about me."

"Well, we've only known each other a few weeks." She still couldn't believe how quickly she'd been certain he was the one for her.

Clearly, if she'd known of his propensity for slowly torturing her to death, she might have given this relationship a little more time. She grinned. No she wouldn't. He always did have a slow hand and enjoyed the journey as much as reaching the destination. That was one of the things she loved most about him.

But he released her all too quickly. Thinking one of them had come to their senses, she prepared to continue their hike along the trail until he pulled her into a nearby wooded area and pressed her back against the trunk of an aspen tree.

"I figure we'll have a lot more privacy here than we will to-night at the campground," he said by way of explanation.

She grinned before he lowered his face to her upturned one. His warm lips nibbled at hers, placing kisses at the corners of her mouth, licking along the crease, begging for admittance. She held out as long as she could before she opened her mouth to his now-insistent tongue. Her desire increased as he kneaded her breast and pinched her nipple. Instantaneous need consumed her, and she reached up to try and remove his leather jacket but only managed to get it down to his elbows.

Ryder pulled away, breathing as hard as she—and not from the high altitude this time. His lascivious smile made her heart skip a few beats. After a moment, he paused to assess their location while she unbuttoned and unzipped her jeans.

"Eager, are we?" he asked.

"I'm just not sure I want an audience of hikers—or wild animals—so I'm being efficient."

"Efficiency has its place, but one of my goals here is to make sure you're vocal enough to scare off any intruders."

Her clit tingled in anticipation as she removed her jacket and handed it to him. She smiled. "I'll do my best, Sir."

He laid both leather side down on the ground in the center of the aspen grove.

Together, they shucked their boots and jeans. The sight of his tented black boxers made her speed up her own disrobing efforts to catch up. Each discarded item of clothing was added to the bed of sorts he was making on the ground. It would still be hard without sleeping bags but he was doing his best to make it comfortable.

"You're on top, Red." She loved when he called her that. "I'll take the ground."

Once again, he thought of her needs ahead of his. She'd have to make the hard ground worth it to him. Megan smiled. "My pleasure."

*   *   *

Megan's impish grin made Ryder even harder. He closed the gap between them. "Raise your arms." She did so, and he lifted

7

her tank over her head, his gaze never leaving hers. He loved that she never wore a bra. One less layer to deal with.

Closing his eyes, he lowered his mouth to one peak and licked her nipple, feeling it harden instantly. Placing his teeth on her, he bit gently and pulled away, taking her with him. She arched her back to follow him, causing him to release her.

"Eyes." She met his gaze, and he pressed her against the aspen trunk. "You are to keep your spine in contact with this tree unless instructed otherwise."

Her pupils dilated. "Yes, Sir."

"Now, where was I?"

"You were torturing my nips, Sir."

He shook his head but couldn't hold back the smile. They hadn't made love in three days. He'd missed having that connection with her, even though she'd been plastered against him on the bike most of that time.

Soon she'd be on top of him, and he'd be buried deep inside her.

Ryder didn't have to worry about restraining her. Megan would stay put, not wanting to risk putting an end to their time together even if it would only postpone the inevitable. Grabbing her hair, he pulled her head back. Dominance surged through him. God, he needed this. Needed her.

He plundered her mouth again, his thumb and index finger rolling the same nipple he'd aroused a moment ago, as he captured her moan in his mouth. His hand roamed over her skin, noting her scars in passing but focused more on reaching the destination at the juncture of her thighs. He broke free of her lips. "Spread your legs. Remember where your spine is to remain."

Megan inched her feet apart, careful to keep her back straight, and he slid his hand inside her panties. Wet. He avoided her clit and delved into her pussy, sinking two fingers deep inside her. When he began pumping in and out, she grabbed onto the slim trunk to steady herself, threw her head back, and panted. He loved watching her responsiveness.

Knowing she was ready for him, he withdrew his hand. "Clean my fingers," he commanded as he held them in front of her mouth. She opened her eyes, now smoky with lust, and maintained eye contact as she took both wet fingers onto her tongue and closed her lips around them.

When she started pumping them in and out as though giving him head, he groaned. Enough foreplay. He pulled his fingers from her mouth and took her hand as he led her toward the quasi-bed he'd made on the ground. "Remove your panties." He watched her slide them over her hips, thighs, and calves before stepping out of them. "Now my boxers." Leaving her panties where they lay, she stepped closer and reached out to hook her thumbs into the waistband, pulling it away from and over his erection. She gave the sensitive knob of his dick a seemingly accidental tweak, but the grin on her face gave her away.

Removing his T-shirt, Ryder laid it down flat on the pile and stretched out on the clothing, crooking his finger for her to join him. She knelt with her knees straddling his calves, and her gaze feasted momentarily on his dick. "Your choice. Suck me, or ride me."

She nibbled the inside of her lower lip as though contemplating a difficult decision. "If you wait too long, I'll take the choice away."

Without further hesitation, she bent over him and took his dick inside her mouth. Just as she'd teased his fingers moments ago, she flicked the knob with her tongue until he fisted his hands trying to keep from coming undone too soon. He wanted this to last as long as possible.

The sound of laughter broke into his thoughts. *Fuck!* He tugged Megan by the hair to lift her mouth off him and drag her body over his. "Shhh," he whispered. "Someone's coming."

*And, unfortunately, it's not Megan or me.*

She giggled softly, but soon became silent, resting her head on his chest as they lay on the ground behind the low growth bushes listening to footsteps on the trail. He wrapped his arms tightly around her, but couldn't really cover her with the discarded clothing underneath them without calling attention to their position. If they remained perfectly still, the hikers might pass them by without a glance, too busy staring at the other Wilson peak.

He couldn't make out how many there were but at least two were a man and a woman. He hoped they didn't get the same idea he and Megan had and wander into the aspen grove to discover them.

"Beautiful," the woman said.

"Told you it was worth the hike," a man responded in a low voice.

Megan began lightly tracing his shoulder to his bicep, then continued down his arm to his forearm and hand until she reached his fingertips. In the same steady motion, she grazed her fingertips down his side to his hip before lifting her hip slightly, reaching between their bodies to seek out his dick.

He couldn't swat her to get her to behave, so he let her have her fun. For now.

The voices of the unsuspecting intruders were drowned out by the blood rushing in his ears. Her fingers grasped his length and stroked him slowly. Clearly, she was trying to get him to groan or otherwise call attention to them. He wouldn't have pegged her for an exhibitionist, but he had better self-control than that.

He forced himself to focus on the nearby hikers who seemed in no hurry to move the fuck on. Megan's tormenting and teasing continued. Man, he owed her big-time for this. Lifting his arm, he reached for her nipple and pinched it, holding it like a clamp to cut off the blood flow. Her hand stilled. No doubt she knew what lay ahead of her when he released it if he held it long enough. Would she be able to maintain *her* composure and stay quiet, or would she bring the hikers rushing in to save her from whatever perceived beast was on the attack?

She lifted her head and stared into his eyes, a quizzical look on her face. Leaning closer to his ear, she whispered, "You sure that's a good idea?"

He held his ground—well, her nip—and smiled. She glanced toward where the hikers' voices had come from and inched up his chest before sliding back down again and easing herself onto his dick. He couldn't see whether they still had company and didn't care, either.

Megan sheathed him inside her silky passage.

He'd died and gone to heaven.

"Mmm." She didn't try to lower her voice. "Feels so good. I've missed you." They'd been unable to find a place to make love for days. He'd missed her, too.

Leveraging herself onto her hands and knees, she pistoned on his dick. Her breasts bounced, but Ryder continued to hold onto the one nipple, pinching it harder. He glanced toward the trail again, but the hikers had either moved on or were silently watching. Maybe they'd learn a thing or two about enjoying nature. He turned his complete attention on his sexy bride.

\* \* \*

Megan watched the hiking couple venture farther along the trail, no longer worried about being discovered, but Ryder didn't seem aware that they'd left, given his nervous glance in that direction.

Letting her hair cascade around either side of his head, she leaned down and kissed him. Being in control and on top of him emboldened her. With more of her weight off his hips now, he began pounding in and out of her to match her pace, occasionally causing friction with her clit, leaving her breathless. Her tongue entered his mouth, claiming him as hers.

That he was her husband still floored her sometimes. But the chemistry between them—in and out of bed—was too powerful to deny. Why waste precious time with a long engagement? Without a doubt, they would be together for a long time.

With his free hand, Ryder reached between their bodies. She broke the kiss and lifted her torso to give him better access, propping herself up on her hands. His penis hit a spot deep inside her that made her legs almost turn to jelly. He filled every inch of her—body and soul. She closed her eyes until his finger began playing with her clit. The combination of stimulating the two bundles of nerves at the same time built tension to a fever pitch.

"Come with me, Red."

She was close, but not quite there yet. Then he released her nipple. Seconds later, as blood rushed back in, she screamed, "Oh, my God!" Pain quickly turned to pleasure as he pumped harder and the world crashed around her. People from two counties could probably hear her screams echoing around the mountains, but she didn't care if every park ranger and hiker in the vicinity came running. All that mattered in this moment was this amazing orgasm. Ryder closed his eyes and grunted as he came with her. She loved watching him in this moment of utter abandon and release.

Exhausted, moments later she collapsed onto his chest again, and he wrapped his arms around her protectively.

"Woman, you're going to kill me before I'm forty."

"Oh, no, Mr. Wilson. I intend to keep you around much longer than a couple of years."

Safe in his arms, she must have dozed, but felt something crawling on her side and swatted it away only to realize it was Ryder's hand.

"Nice nap?"

"Sorry. I didn't even realize I was sleepy."

"Great sex can have that effect. But don't worry. I kept watch while you were out. Those two hikers wandered by fifteen minutes ago. It's probably safe for us to get dressed now."

Megan hated to leave her perch. "I hope I haven't crushed you."

"You're light as a feather, although I think my arm might have fallen asleep." He shook it to return the feeling before she reached down to grab the offended extremity and help him up.

He pulled some wipes from the backpack and cleaned her thighs and a couple more for himself, and they brushed off their clothing to dress. Her hips had been stretched wide for so long, she wasn't sure she could walk. They exited the woods and stood on the path.

"Which way?" she asked.

Ryder glanced at the setting sun. "Gets dark early in the mountains. I'd say we'd best head back to camp."

She nodded, took his hand, and they strolled side by side when possible. The campground opened up before them alongside the lake. A couple riding horses caught their eye. "Magnificent creatures." Megan pulled her SLR from the backpack and snapped some images.

"I haven't been around horses much, being from Chicago. How about you?"

He shook his head. When the horses and riders ventured closer, Megan struck up a conversation with the woman. "Are they friendly?"

"Mine is. His can be a little skittish around strangers."

Megan reached out to stroke the neck of the spotted one under the woman. "Mustang?"

The woman nodded. "Both are rescue horses."

They discussed the horse's abusive background and what it had taken to reach this point after a couple years of work.

Suddenly, Megan realized Ryder had been awfully quiet and turned to see him standing in front of the other horse. The two seemed locked in silent communication, but the horse showed no signs of panic or unease with Ryder.

"I see he's been around horses a bit," the female rider commented.

"Actually, I don't think so." Megan marveled at Ryder's relaxed stance. He seemed lost in a place far removed from her and the others around him. She didn't want to intrude so remained silent, watching.

After a few minutes, he pulled himself out of the spell and his body stiffened, instantly back on alert. He glanced at her, then at the two riders. "Beautiful animal."

"Thanks." The riders clicked their tongues and squeezed their knees against the sides of the horses and went on their way.

"I thought you said you hadn't spent much time around horses."

"I haven't. Man, that was weird. I felt such a strong connection to the horse in that moment. And a sense that somehow horses would be part of my destiny."

She grinned. "I'm not sure how, but I've learned not to ignore those feelings. One thing for sure, I've never seen you so relaxed. The woman said that horse was usually skittish around strangers, but you two really hit it off."

He shook his head, and they continued toward the bike to unload and set up camp.

She suddenly knew she needed to find this man some horses to connect with but was unsure how to make that happen.

# Ryder & Megan:
# Finding their Destiny

Megan stared at Ryder on her right, then at Luke Denton seated at the table to her left. A month after their honeymoon, she couldn't believe how much had happened. But had she heard correctly? "You're offering to sell us your ranch house, Luke? But you love this place."

"It's the ranch and horses I love, not the house. And everything pales in comparison to how much I love Cassie. She's a mountain girl at heart, and I need to get her and her alpacas back up on Iron Horse Peak as soon as possible."

Ryder chimed in, "I've agreed to help Luke build their new house."

Luke leaned on his forearms, closing the space between the three of them. "It goes without saying, but this discussion remains between the three of us. If Cassie gets wind of it, she'll put an end to my plans right quick."

Ryder added, "Cassie's place was destroyed by a wildfire this summer. While he and I are busy with the build, we may need you to divert Cassie so she won't suspect anything."

"Of course. I'll help any way I can. I enjoy Cassie's company." She smiled at Luke, idly scratching Chance behind the ears. Kachina, the puppy they were adopting from Chance's litter, nudged her ankle begging to be held. She reached down to oblige. "I won't say a word."

The thought of them living on this peaceful ranch with Luke's

15

horses was like an answer to a prayer. The spirit world must have been busy aligning the perfect life for them. Ryder had already spent a lot of time learning the ropes, so to speak, from Luke as to how to care for the horses just in the brief time they'd been out here on their extended honeymoon. For the first time, they had some inkling of where they might want to settle down, but she and Ryder had a lot to talk about before making the decision.

Then Luke quoted a purchase price far below what she would expect a house and a few acres of land must go for here. She raised her eyebrows, yet he seemed serious.

"It's a fair price, Megan, given that Ryder's going to work off a good portion of the property value over the next month or so while on the build site. I've offered him a job overseeing things here at the ranch after the house is finished, too. Having people I can trust when I can't be here will give me peace of mind."

She reached onto the table to squeeze Ryder's hand. "Looks like we're not going to have to go house hunting after all," she began before turning toward Luke again, "which is a good thing because we had no clue where we wanted to settle down."

"You're okay with it?" Ryder asked. "I was going to talk it over with you tonight, but things are moving fast."

"I think our hasty wedding established the fact neither of us is one to mull things over incessantly. Sometimes you have to go for the gusto and worry about the consequences later." She saw no down side to this opportunity. "Besides, we both love it up here and can't live in Carlos's house forever." Megan kissed him.

When they pulled away, he said, "I love you, Red."

The bundle of fluff on her lap stirred and she bent to nuzzle Kachina's fur. Using the puppy's nickname, she said, "Soon I won't have to leave you here without me anymore, Chee." She hated leaving her behind the last couple of nights.

His grin told her Ryder was happy about that, too. "Who'd have thought when I saw those horses while camping at Woods

16

Lake that we'd be taking care of some this soon?" He turned toward Luke. "I know I have a lot to learn, but I think I have an affinity with the animals."

"You sure as hell do. After seeing you with O'Keeffe and Fontana, I knew you'd be perfect."

Megan loved that Luke had named his horses after famous artists, being one himself. And that he was so supportive.

"Working with your horses calms me. It's just what I need right now."

She'd have been blind not to notice how relaxed he'd become since arriving here. They'd come for a family picnic with Adam's expanded family a couple of days ago and hadn't been able to tear themselves away since. Last night, they'd camped near the creek, listening to the water gurgling past them and staring up at the millions of stars. They'd probably do the same tonight.

"Megan," Ryder said, "Luke and I have some special plans for the future of this place that I'll share with you later tonight."

Luke stood. "Why don't you two join us for dinner? Cassie always makes enough food for an army."

Megan glanced at Ryder who shook his head imperceptibly. They'd made plans to have dinner in Fairchance, and she was anxious to hear what else these two men were cooking up. "I think we'll take a rain check," Megan told Luke.

"Anytime. Now, if you'll excuse me, I need to get back to the house. Ryder, let's head up to Iron Horse Peak tomorrow morning after the horses are taken care of. I'd like your input on some construction decisions."

"Sure, man."

Megan smiled as she returned Kachina to her mama and gathered up her purse. In a very short time, she and Ryder had made new friends, but most importantly, he'd found a job and a purpose in life. Working with Luke would be perfect, helping him avoid the triggers of big cities and crowds.

They left the workshop and headed for the Harley. Ryder walked the bike away from the barn area before kick-starting it. She donned her helmet and jumped on before scooting herself to the back of the seat. While Luke and Cassie had offered to let them stay with them, the house only had one bedroom and she didn't want to intrude. They had the barn's tack room if the weather turned bad, but she'd come to love sleeping in their small tent, cuddled together and staring up through the "window" in the top at the stars.

Over dinner at the vintage hotel, she discussed with him some ideas for jumpstarting her own career. The nearest city was Breckenridge, only thirty minutes away. If there wasn't a glut of photography studios there already—and a quick search of the internet would tell her that—her easiest option would be opening one that catered to a year-round mix of locals and tourists.

Her dad must be smiling down from heaven, pleased with how she intended to spend some of her trust fund income on a house and a small studio.

As they shared a dessert, their conversation returned once more to what Ryder and Luke had planned. "He's thinking about putting in some bunkhouses for guests. Not a dude ranch, though. We want to create an immersion program for people like me having trouble with PTSD—as well as those with physical disabilities or psychological traumas—where they can spend time with the animals and find a source of peace and maybe even a new purpose."

"That sounds like a wonderful idea!" Cassie had told her how the horses had helped her in many ways, too. Sharing that healing with others would be phenomenal. "Maybe I can take some photos and help set up a web site."

He smiled at her, reaching across the table to hold her hand. "Thanks for being so supportive of everything I do."

"I love this idea and am honored to be a part of it."

After dinner, with the sun lower on the horizon, they rode back to the ranch and out toward the creek on a roadway Luke used for his truck. The ranch was beautiful, small by the standards she knew from western movies, but for this city girl, the open spaces made her feel as though they were two of the few people remaining on earth.

Pulling up to the flat rock area where they'd camped last night, they'd soon pitched their tent and tossed their sleeping bags inside. They wouldn't unroll them until they were ready to crawl inside. She'd learned that early in this trip—that a sleeping bag unrolled too early accumulated a lot of moisture from the dew and became a haven for bugs.

She smiled, wondering what Patrick would think if he saw her roughing it like this. My, how her life had changed in the past two months. Adam sending Ryder to check on her the night of the break-in at her studio had changed both their lives forever.

\*   \*   \*

After making love, Ryder held Megan, her head resting on his chest, as he stared out through the opening in the tent's roof. Somehow, those stars had suddenly aligned to take years of misery away and turn his life around—well, the stars aligned with Megan, a force to be reckoned with.

"When will you start working on the house?" she asked, drawing him back.

"We've already drawn up the plans, so any day. The first building materials should be delivered tomorrow, so I plan on spending the day up there waiting on them."

"I'm sure it's gorgeous. If you won't need me, I'll make myself scarce and take some photos. Perhaps I can find some shots that can be used for the décor later on."

"Cassie and Luke would like that. Sounds good. With all the hands we'll have to unload, I doubt I'll need you. But once we get started, I may recruit you. Handy with a hammer?"

"I'm teachable." She plucked idly at the hairs on his chest. "It might be fun working with you on this. Patrick never let me do anything when we were kids, although my mom usually made him include me."

"My sister and I were pretty much left to our own devices, but she had no interest in the projects I was involved in during my late teens."

"Does Marcia know you're moving to Colorado?"

"Not yet. It took a whole day for me to even tell you. She's witnessed enough of the failures in my life that I don't care to add to the list."

"She loves you. A lot. I didn't get the impression when we were in Santa Fe that she judged you as harshly as you do yourself. Marcia wants you to be happy and fulfilled again."

He shrugged. "You're the one whose opinion matters most. I wanted to think through every angle and make sure this was right for us both before getting your hopes up, too. Everything's been happening so fast with us. I guess I keep waiting for it all to blow up in my face."

Megan leaned up on her elbow and stared down at him, although he could only see the silhouette of her head with the moon as backlighting. "I told you before I'll be happy wherever you are. You also know I'm versatile enough in my career choice to be able to bloom wherever I'm planted." She traced her finger down the stubble on his jaw. "I feel in my heart this is where we're meant to be at this point in time. Well, not here by this creek," she grinned, "but living on this ranch. The horses, especially. I had no clue how horses could possibly enter into our lives—and now look at you. Amazing things are going to happen here, Ryder. I can feel it to the depths of my soul."

He hoped she was right. His decision to marry Megan after being together such a short time had him worried, but he was gaining confidence in that decision every day. This decision felt right as well.

"What do you think your brother's going to say?"

"Patrick?"

"No. He took the wedding calmly enough, so I'm not worried too much about him. I mean Adam." Facing his former master sergeant last month to tell him he'd married the man's little sister after knowing her only a couple of weeks had been one of the most stressful things he'd faced since Fallujah.

"I guess I don't see the same man you and the others who served under him do. I really didn't know him growing up, either. Mom always idolized him as if he could do nothing wrong. I'll admit, there were times as a teen when I was more than a little envious that he was forever suspended in a bubble of perfection from the moment he ran away at sixteen, unlike me who gave Mom daily reminders that I'm a flawed child of hers."

She sighed, and he wondered how they'd grown so close given that she'd only known him for less than a year.

"Sorry. Didn't mean to go there. But I love both of my brothers; I just don't give them power over me. Adam also treats women differently, so I may never see what you guys do. But he's been nothing but supportive of our being together. Of course, I don't know what the two of you discussed when I wasn't there. However, you ought to know that he expects me to run to him if I ever have any trouble with you." She laughed and tapped his nose. "Don't you worry, though, Ryder. I'll take care of you myself if you ever get out of line."

"I'll hold you to that, Red." He wasn't prone to violence, but what about accidentally or inadvertently hurting her?

"You'll also be harder on yourself than I could ever be."

"True."

Ryder placed his hand at the nape of her neck and drew her to him for a kiss. He'd intended it to be chaste, but she ignited a

21

flame inside him once more. Not that he could do anything about it this soon, but he sure as hell could bring Megan to another orgasm.

*Enough serious talk.* "I'm going to make you scream again in a few minutes."

Her voice grew husky. "I just came. Give a girl time to recover."

He lightly brushed his fingertips over her arms from her shoulders to her wrists and back again. "Maybe we need to do a little warming up, while I tell you everything I intend to do to your beautiful naked body."

He skimmed his hands over her back on his upward journey. "First, I'm going to touch every sexy inch of you, nice and slowly like this until you reach the point where you're begging me to touch you…" He reached between their bodies to the juncture of her thighs and squeezed hard, but fleetingly. "Here."

Her breath hitched, and she braced her hands on his chest.

"But not yet. No. I still have a lot of territory to cover before we get there."

"Damn you, but you already have me wanting to beg. How do you do that?"

He chuckled. "Naturally gifted, I suppose." He slapped her butt. "Now, focus, Red."

"I will if you slap me harder."

His cock stirred. Hell, maybe he wasn't finished for the night after all. "Face down over my lap." He sat up and guided her into place, stroking her ass and thighs before squeezing her luscious globes to heighten the sensation of what was to come.

*Slap! Slap!*

He landed one smack on each ass cheek. She squirmed in a way he knew meant she wanted more. Brushing his hands over her skin again, he let his finger trail between her crack to rub the area between her star opening and her pussy. They hadn't tried anal and he wondered if that would be her thing, but they definitely weren't prepared for that tonight.

Her throaty moan made him hornier.

*Slap! Slap!*

He rained a dozen more blows onto her cheeks and upper thighs in rapid succession until she squirmed to avoid his hand. *Oh, no, baby. I'm not finished yet.* Spanking her hadn't been among his original plans, so he rolled her onto her back and took a hard nipple between his teeth, pulling until she arched her back. Kissing it, he moved to the other, only for this one, he alternately sucked and flicked his tongue against the stiffening peak. Her hands went to the back of his head to hold him in place, but he pulled away.

"Tsk, tsk. Who's in charge of this fantasy?"

"You are, Sir."

"Remember that." He grinned, knowing she could probably see his face in the moonlight but not caring. "And if you try to manipulate this scene with your hands again, I'll tie you to the tent spike."

"Promises, promises."

He pinched her side, shaking his head. How'd he find such a brat? *Yeah, who are you trying to kid?* He enjoyed the hell out of her brattiness every time. They wouldn't be this carefree forever, so he'd sure as hell make the most of their honeymoon period.

"I'm going to use my tongue and teeth to bring you to the edge multiple times before I let you come." He kissed her again on the mouth and continued his slow arousal of her senses, spending a lot of time kissing and nibbling her neck, loving the moans she made. But he didn't remain there so long she could grow accustomed to or anticipate his actions. Instead, he made forays to her shoulders and the hollow at the side of her neck periodically, avoiding her nipples and pussy for the moment.

Out here, she could be as loud as she wanted, and no one

would come running. He loved hearing her scream her release, but if he postponed gratification, she'd enjoy it even more—as would he.

Homing in on her nipple again—he'd never get enough of them—his lips and teeth tormented her while his hand roamed over her abdomen, lower and lower, but still not touching her where she wanted him. His cock became stiffer. He was insatiable when it came to his beautiful bride.

\* \* \*

Megan's body burned for the man beside her, now more than ever. Would she ever reach the point where she was sated and unable to be turned on again?

Doubtful. Not for their first few decades anyway.

His lips teased her nipple to the point of aching, leaving her wanting so much more. To keep from inadvertently grabbing or manipulating him, she lifted her hands above her head and pretended she was in restraints. While they'd had some imaginative lovemaking while camping, she missed being tied to a bed. Call her old-fashioned.

She tamped down a giggle, which would be wholly inappropriate at the moment. A pinch to her hip told her he knew she wasn't focused, so she pushed all other thoughts aside and let him worship her body. He trailed kisses over her abdomen to her navel where he licked her. She cringed, that area being less than erogenous given her surgery. But he didn't seem focused on her scars and couldn't see them anyway.

*Focus.*

His hand stroked her thighs, parting her legs. *Here we go.*

But he only teased her, glancing off her pussy hairs but not touching her there. He knelt beside her and continued the path his lips had started, over her hipbone and toward her knee, pausing for a nibble or two on her inner thigh. She spread her legs wider, but he didn't take the hint. Instead, he kissed the inside of her knee, surprising her at how sensual it felt, then kissed the other. She realized she'd been holding her breath and let it out in a gasp.

Ryder spread her legs wider and crawled between them, facing her, but instead of homing in on the place she most wanted him, he scooted backward until he placed a kiss on her ankle. She still wore her no-show socks because she didn't want her feet to be cold. He'd never paid any attention to her feet and toes before, but this time, he removed first one, then the other.

*This can't be good.*

When he kissed her instep, she recoiled. While not ticklish, she wasn't sure she wanted to have him kissing her feet.

"I thought you weren't ticklish on your feet."

"I'm not. It's just...I'm not sure how clean my feet are for kissing."

He chuckled. "We were wading in the creek a while ago. They're fine." Ryder pulled her leg by the ankle, cradling her foot in both hands as he kissed the same spot. A jolt of electricity zinged straight to her clit. Perhaps he'd discovered a new erogenous zone. Knowing he had no issues with her feet, she shed her unease and gave in to the feelings.

But he soon moved away from her feet and blazed a trail of kisses up the insides of both her legs. The slight stubble from his scruff only added to the delicious sensations he sparked along the way, but when he crooked his forearms around her thighs and spread her open, she held her breath.

*Finally!*

Only he seemed intent upon driving her slowly insane, because he focused everywhere but on her clit. He nibbled at her lower lips, blew on her clit hood, and toyed with the opening of her pussy. She tilted her pelvis to give him better access, but he *still* avoided her clit.

"Ryder, honey, I need to come!"

The vibration of his chuckle reverberated through her. He pulled away. "Good to know. Because I need to make you come. I'm just not ready yet."

She groaned, and he went back to his slow torture. He'd probably make her wait even longer now because she'd begged. Not that he hadn't wanted exactly that response from her, no doubt.

When his tongue flicked the outside of her hood, her hips bucked involuntarily. She willed them to remain still, intensifying the feelings and improving his aim.

*Please, oh, please, Ryder!*

How much more could she take without him giving her the release she needed? She wished it hadn't been so soon after Ryder came, because she wanted to feel him buried deep inside her again, too. But he told her it would take him a few hours to be ready for more. Maybe she'd wake him up in the middle of the night for more. She had a hard time sleeping on the ground with the night noises outside anyway, so would surely awaken at some...

Ryder bit the inside of her thigh, bringing her back to the moment. *Focus on one orgasm at a time.*

How'd she become so insatiable? Because she had a lover who cared about her needs. Luckily, she hadn't wasted her time on any others, but her friends had certainly complained enough about their experiences.

When he moved one hand so that two of his fingers could spread her outer lips and pull them apart, the cold evening air coupled with Ryder's warm breath brought every sense to high alert.

*Don't anticipate.*

Hadn't he been trying to train her to stay in the moment? Wanting to show him she'd been listening, she grasped the edge of the tent and concentrated solely on his attentions.

Her reward was the further building up of tension as he teased her without mercy, venturing ever so close before veering off in another direction. Each time she thought he'd take her over the edge, he'd nibble or lick her somewhere else. As his tongue dipped inside her pussy, she took a breath before the next assault. Her clit was so much more sensitive.

The combination of driving his finger into her and his tongue flicking the sides of her clit hood nearly made her lose her mind. When he pulled back her hood, she waited.

*Please, Ryder!*

Sweat broke out on her forehead and down her back. This damp sleeping bag wouldn't be very comfortable to sleep in tonight. But a little discomfort would be worth it.

When he stroked her G-spot and sucked her clit between his lips, her knees grew too weak to keep up. He pumped in and out of her more rapidly, and then surprised the hell out of her by mounting her, his hard cock driving into her in one smooth motion. "Oh!"

"I didn't think—"

"I don't want you to think. Just feel."

Oh, she felt him all right. He pulled out and plunged into her again, this time taking his finger and stroking her clit to keep her riding the crest as he increased the tempo. Needing to hang on, she placed her hands on his shoulders and felt his muscles ripple with the exertion.

"So tight, baby. So damned good."

Tilting her pelvis to give him deeper access, she matched his rhythm. Both of them grunted with each thrust. She was so close, but waited for him. "Come first, Red. I'm right behind you." He draped her legs over his shoulders and pounded into her, hitting her G-spot while also touching her clit until the air in the tent exploded around them as did she.

"Oh, God! Yes!" She couldn't see his face, but didn't have to in order to know he was smiling as he always did when he gave her an orgasm.

He increased the pace of his movements and grunted when he came. When he stopped, he nearly collapsed onto her. His weight was so welcome that she wrapped her arms and legs around him and cuddled him.

Tears sprang to her eyes at the magnitude of what they'd shared tonight. "That was incredible. But I may not be able to walk for a week."

"No problem. I'll carry you. Now, let's do a little moonlight skinny-dipping and clean off."

"Are you crazy? That mountain stream will be frigid."

"No worries. I'm definitely finished for the night."

Megan smiled. *That's what you think, my darling hubby.*

# Ryder & Megan:
# Leather and Daisies

Ryder followed Gunnar Larson into his office compound in Breckenridge. The man towered over him, his long blond hair in a sleek ponytail down to the middle of his back. Getting into the man's inner sanctum had taken several pre-screenings as well as two security checks on the premises. One would think he'd been trying to scale the walls of Fort Knox.

Ryder wasn't even here to discuss business. He'd asked to meet at the man's dungeon, but because that was in his home, apparently, he preferred to make initial contact at the Forseti Group headquarters. Of course, with his involvement in black ops and paramilitary contracting, Ryder understood the need for caution.

He'd met Gunnar more than a month ago at the family barbecue at Luke's place. Hard to imagine, but now this house belonged to Ryder and Megan. Anyway, he'd learned of Gunnar's reputation for being the best whip master in the area. After talking with Megan and seeing her interest in having him learn to throw a whip, he'd gotten contact info from Luke and asked to do some training under Gunnar.

"Have a seat, Ryder."

Setting his coffee mug on a coaster on the imposing wooden desk, Ryder sat down in the chair on the right. "Thanks for taking the time to meet with me."

"No problem. I'm always pleased to provide training to other

Doms who want to learn respect for and the many uses of various whips. Tell me exactly what skill you'd like to learn first."

"The bullwhip. Nothing hardcore, but Megan and I are interested in trying butterfly kisses—nothing that would mark her skin long-term."

"Tagging, but not marking."

"I'm not familiar with the terminology. We haven't played at a dungeon yet."

Gunnar stared at him a long, uncomfortable moment, as if sizing him up. "I know you served with Adam Montague, and you're his brother-in-law, but I had to do some checking into your background before inviting you in here."

"I've heard."

"Oh?"

Ryder explained, "Grant gave me a heads-up that you were checking me out."

Gunnar smiled. "She's loyal to her friends."

"I wouldn't say we're friends, but we served together, and she figured she owed me one."

Gunnar cocked his brow, but Ryder wasn't going to talk about Grant's breach of trust involving Megan. Suffice it to say, she'd been making amends ever since. Besides, if not for her actions, he'd have never met Megan, so it was difficult to hold a grudge.

Gunnar nodded. "Understandable. So...back to learning to throw a whip. You've checked out and I'd like to invite you both to my dungeon party day after tomorrow. Another couple you know will be there—Marc and Angelina."

He'd hoped for a private lesson first, in case he was inept with a whip, but Megan would find out soon enough. Otherwise, they knew so few people around here, they had nothing to worry about. If people didn't accept them for who they were, then to hell with them.

Gunnar reached for a set of papers beside him. "Take these

two application forms, and each of you fill one out. Bring them with you. There's a map to my place on the last page. Remember, confidentiality is expected. You don't talk about what goes on in the dungeon with anyone who isn't a member."

He didn't know many people in the area and had no clue who was a member or not other than Marc and Angelina.

"I think I can probably teach you enough that first night and let you practice for a couple of days before I have you out again to check your form. But don't you dare go near Megan with a whip until I give you the go-ahead. We're going to work on precision and targeting first, nice and gentle. If you two decide you want a little more power later on, we can work on that, too. But I like that you're starting out slowly. Now, why don't we schedule the follow-ups, too, before the schedule gets too tight."

"Evenings are best for me, too, because the ranch work keeps me busy during the day."

"Perfect." Gunnar jotted down handed him a slip of paper with the evenings he was available for two more sessions in the week to come, Ryder discussed where would be the best place to purchase a single tail, and Gunnar even pulled out some instructions on the oiling and caring for a new whip.

Gunnar stood and Ryder did likewise. They shook hands. "I'm looking forward to seeing you and Megan at the party."

"Oh, how should we dress?"

"Comfortably. If that means kink clothing, fine, but if you're more comfortable in jeans and a t-shirt like me"—Gunnar indicated his casual attire—"go for it."

\*     \*     \*

Megan had butterflies clawing to get out of her stomach as she and Ryder walked into Gunnar's residence through a special entrance. The darkened room was lit with flickering wall sconces simulating fire, and her gaze roamed the room, taking in the various stations with some familiar and some bizarre equipment.

"Can I get you something to drink?"

She didn't expect to be doing any intensive scenes on their first visit but would be cautious anyway. "A water with lemon would be great. Thanks."

"I'll turn in our forms, too." As Ryder walked over to the bar, Megan took in her surroundings. What would her brothers think to find out she'd gone to a BDSM club? Well, they didn't have to know everything about her.

She spotted a St. Andrew's cross, which immediately captured her attention. She'd dreamed of being bound to one ever since reading about it in *Club Shadowlands*, the first BDSM romance she'd ever read.

She'd chosen a thin layer of clothing in order to experience whatever Ryder wanted to try tonight after his bullwhip lesson was over.

As her eyes adjusted better, she saw movement to her right and turned to see Angelina Giardano approaching. While they'd only met twice, Megan liked her a lot and wanted to get to know her better.

"Megan! Welcome! I'm so glad to see you're into this, too."

"Well, we're trying to learn more about it. This is my first time in a club other than in books."

"Gunnar's is a great private place to play, although we'd stopped coming while I was getting my restaurant started. Living in Aspen Corners and working here, this is so much more convenient, although we try to get to the Masters at Arms once a month or so."

"I haven't heard of that one. Where's it located?"

Angelina's eyes widened. "Oh, it's just a little place in Denver. Not one you'd want to bother going to since you're living out here."

Her response seemed strange, but Megan didn't really know

the woman all that well. "Ryder and I are just beginning to get settled in but are dying to come and try your restaurant. I'm hearing good things."

Angelina beamed. "Let me know ahead of time, and I'll prepare a memorable special that night." Being a chef was her calling, apparently.

"I have a feeling *all* of your dishes will be memorable."

"And you would be correct." Marc D'Alessio approached. "Hi, Megan." He wrapped his arm around Angelina's waist and smiled down at her. "This woman puts an amazing amount of love and care into each dish she makes."

Ryder arrived with their bottles of water. "Megan and I need to come to your place soon."

"My thought exactly," Megan agreed.

The crack of a bullwhip made Megan jump, then laugh self-consciously.

"Sounds like Gunnar's planning to play tonight," Marc said. "He's usually much quieter with the single tail."

"Actually, that might be for our benefit. That's why we're here. He's going to train me to throw one."

Marc nodded. "You couldn't ask for a better instructor." He glanced down at Angelina. "Maybe you'd be interested in that someday, too?"

She shook her head. "I doubt it. Let's stick to the Florentine floggers."

Marc grinned. "My pleasure, *cara*." Turning his attention to Ryder and Megan again, he said, "If you'll excuse us, there's a cross over there awaiting my lady's pleasure."

Megan was tempted to follow and watch, but Gunnar walked up to them at that moment. "Glad you made it. I think we're all set. Megan, Ryder has asked for a demonstration first." He had? "How would you feel about being my target tonight?"

She glanced at Ryder who smiled. "Totally up to you, but I

33

thought we ought to see if you really enjoy this kind of play first. It's probably going to take me weeks of practice before we can try anything ourselves."

Staring up at Gunnar again, she wondered what it would be like. She'd been curious since Ryder had asked her. His intense stare sent a shiver up her spine, but Ryder was here to keep an eye on things, and she'd spelled out her hard limits precisely on the form she'd filled out. But it was never a bad idea to confirm when negotiating with someone who might not have seen the form yet.

She smiled. "I'm good with it."

Gunnar grinned. "Judging by the way your ponytail jumped a few minutes ago when I cracked the popper, we're going to start with something easy and painless. Excuse me for a few minutes while I look over your form briefly."

When he came back, he led her over to the large area devoid of equipment or furniture. No doubt he needed a wide space to throw the whip without hitting unintended targets. Only, at the moment, she would be the bulls-eye.

"First, because I can't see your body with your clothing on…"

Surely he didn't intend for her to strip naked. She looked at Ryder, whose attention had shifted to Gunnar as well. He didn't seem at all happy about the prospect, either.

"…I'll need to confirm some things and ask some additional questions before we begin. First, are there any medical conditions I should be made aware of? Any skin grafts, superficial injuries in targeted impact areas on your back, ass, or thighs?"

"I can't think of anything that might be a problem in that area, but…" She felt awkward about telling someone she barely knew this, but didn't want to withhold information that might be important. "I had a hysterectomy when I was twenty-four."

Gunnar's brow shot up, but he masked his surprise again quickly. "Any recent impact play?"

Again her gaze went to Ryder, and she smiled before giving

Gunnar her attention again. "Spankings, paddlings—and a run-in with a riding crop. We haven't taken anything to extreme, though, if that's what you mean."

He turned to Ryder who nodded.

Gunnar addressed her again. "Your safeword is scarlet?"

"Yes, Sir."

"Got it. Now, stand here and put your hands over your head, clasping them." She did as instructed, and he stepped back. He curled the whip and threw it in her direction, making it pop just to her left. Her heart felt as though it jumped into her throat, but when he repeated the move again to her right, she managed to hold still a little better. "Well done."

She glanced over at Ryder who nodded and smiled.

"Now I want you to feel the whip on your body. Are you ready?"

Probably not, but she replied, "Yes."

He grew somber, and the next thing she remembered, the whip was hurling toward her. However, instead of striking her with a sting, it wrapped around her waist in more of a hug. "Amazing!" She turned to Ryder again. "Definitely have him teach you that, Sir!"

Ryder chuckled. "Will do, brat."

She shrugged, but decided she ought to be on higher protocol while here so as not to make her Dom look bad in front of the others.

"Ryder," Gunnar said, motioning him over, "just as with a flogger or any other implement you intend to use, you'll want to warm her up slowly, letting the whip caress her skin, both in places you plan to impact as well as others. Here."

He handed the coiled whip to Ryder, who took it, walked around behind her, and rubbed the whip across her shoulders and shoulder blades and then down the hollow of her spine. The smell of leather excited her nearly as much as its touch. He circled around in front again, uncurling the whip. Holding onto the handle with his left hand, he grabbed a spot near the other end of the four-foot braided leather with his right. He stretched the whip taut with a snap before brushing it lightly over her collarbone and upper breasts. Each time he came near her nipples, when her anticipation for the feel of it on her sensitive peaks was at its most intense, he moved back up again and started over. Finally, after several repetitions, he stopped teasing her and rubbed the leather up and down directly over her nipples, only leaving her ready to beg for more.

He grinned. Couldn't he tell she was close to crumpling into a puddle at his feet? He always read her arousal and other moods so well. When her breath became shallow and rapid, he proceeded down and over her abdomen to her thighs encased in black leggings. Though she'd tried to prepare for anything tonight, she hadn't expected to be included in Ryder's lesson like this.

Continuing his slow tease over her body, he looped the whip around her left thigh and ran it slowly up her inner thigh, coming painfully close to her pussy before sliding it down her right inner thigh. She wanted to scream, or grab his hand and guide it where she wanted him to be. As if aware of her thought, Gunnar stepped around behind her and took her by the elbows, guiding her hands into a box hold behind her back.

She drew a shaky breath. Having two men dominating her at the same time had her senses on overload. Feeling the heat of the two men only ignited the flames inside her even more.

Ryder reached between her legs to give Gunnar the end of the whip and then stood tall again in front of her, smiling. "Your pupils are dilated, breathing rapid. I think you're going to have a love affair with the whip, Red."

"Oh, Sir, we're already quite fond of one another."

He chuckled. "Then I think it's time for the two of you to become better acquainted." As if the two men had exchanged some silent signal, both lifted the whip at the same time until she straddled it. The braided leather pressed between her outer lips and against her clit. When they began sawing it back and forth, she gasped in surprise. Each bump of the whip's braids over her oversensitive nerves felt like a flick against her clit until she shook on the inside with suppressed need.

They increased the rhythm until she trembled visibly. Just when she thought she might have to ask for permission to come, they stopped, and she tried not to collapse. Ryder closed the gap between them and kissed her before whispering in her ear, "Red, you're making me so fucking hot."

"Oh, Sir, you don't know the half of how hot I am right now."

He took his free hand and rubbed between her legs, and she sucked in her breath when he touched her, trying not to lose it. "Judging by your response just now, I have a pretty good idea."

"Well done, Ryder," Gunnar said. "I can already tell you're going to be a natural with the whip—and make this little sub quite happy." He tugged playfully at her ponytail. "You can release your arms now. Shake them out."

Without waiting for her to do so, Gunnar walked over to a table where a grocery-store bouquet of daisies had been placed on the table. He tore away the cellophane and broke off three blossoms on three- or four-inch stems before approaching her again.

"Stretch out your arms from your sides and parallel to the floor." She did so, and he placed a flower in each hand, with her fingertips holding the stems and the blooms protruding outward. He didn't step away. Instead, he held out the third one in front of her face. "Open your mouth and take the end of the stem between your teeth."

Her brow wrinkling in confusion, she did as he told her. "Good girl. I've taken away your ability to speak your safeword, but if you need to stop at any point, just drop one of the flowers and give me a thumbs down sign."

Megan nodded her understanding.

Taking his mark in about the same place as he'd thrown the whip before, Gunnar sent the whip hurling toward her, cracking the popper to her left. She jumped, but not nearly as much as she had the first time. Then, an instant later, he did so on her right. She held tightly onto the three daisies, although she nearly bit through the one between her teeth. Adjusting it with her lips and teeth again, she tried to prepare for whatever he intended to do next, but the man was unpredictable.

"Good job, Megan. You're already showing better control of your body's natural responses than you did earlier this evening." At least now she was halfway expecting the sound, although he still seemed to try to catch her off guard. Yet his praise empowered her. She glanced across the space at Ryder, who once again stood out of range of the whip. His nod and smile of approval melted her insides.

"Before we continue, I want you to take a few deep, cleansing breaths—in through your nose and out through your mouth."

She closed her eyes and filled her lungs slowly, then released the air at an equal pace watching the flower petals flutter as she exhaled. After the third complete round, most of the tension had left her body. Megan nodded her readiness, deciding to let her eyes remain closed.

"Open your eyes open and focus on me," Gunnar commanded, and she obeyed. "I want you to become accustomed to seeing the whip hurling toward you so that, over time, your natural reflex to flinch or jerk will go away. Only then will you be a safe target for your Dom to play with." She hadn't thought about how her unpredictable movements would make this unsafe for them both.

"Now, I want to show you there's little to worry about in the hands of someone trained to throw a whip. Of course, I should warn you there have been instances when a whip has become inexplicably tangled."

Her heart pounded. She thought he was an expert.

Ryder asked, "What happened?"

"Let's just say the popper struck the target in a less than opti-mal way. Feels like a bee sting, really. I've had it happen to me more than you will because I train a lot of people and am often their practice target. But you need to know it can happen, even with a whip master who has twenty or more years of experience. There are risks inherent in this type of play and many others. With practice, though, you'll minimize them." He turned to Megan. "The pain lingers only briefly—and the mark may last an hour or two—but even so, there won't be any welts or cuts. Not the way I throw a whip, anyway. Or the way I'll be teaching your Dom to do so. I am aware that you aren't interested in being marked long-term." Did she detect a hint of disappointment in his voice?

"By the time I allow Ryder to do whip play with you, he'll be well versed in all of the safety precautions and an expert with great precision." He turned toward Ryder. "Otherwise, I won't give you the go-ahead to use the whip on her. Understood?"

Ryder nodded. She had no doubt her husband and Dom would take this as seriously as he did every other safety aspect he used when they played.

Now she hoped to keep from flinching when Gunnar hurled the whip her way again.

\*     \*     \*

Ryder's pride in Megan abounded. Almost unflinching in just a matter of minutes. He wished he'd started his training weeks ago and would be the one wielding the whip tonight, but he also wanted to make sure he knew what he was doing before going anywhere near her with one, except for the incredibly sexy introduction to the whip he'd given her moments ago. His lady loved leather, especially when it came in the form of a braided bullwhip.

Gunnar turned to him and gave him some instructions on what to watch as he prepared. Forcing himself to pay close attention to the man's hand, wrist, and whip, Ryder watched him spring into action.

*Crack!*

He moved so quickly, Ryder was left wondering what he'd done. He glanced back at Megan, one flower in her mouth, another in her right hand, but in her left, only a stem remained. Ryder's attention went to the floor where the head of the daisy lay snipped off but otherwise undamaged.

"Incredible." Would he learn to do that without hurting Megan or completely missing the target? Damn, he intended to if he had to practice in the round pen every night and spare moment. The look of awe on Megan's face would be worth every minute.

"Let me slow it down for you this time," Gunnar said. Addressing Megan, he said, "Just hold that pose. We'll be with you again in no time."

Placing the handle in Ryder's hand, Gunnar showed him by guiding him through the paces how to get the whip to curl and roll toward the target—thin air, in his case—and let him practice several times until he, too, could throw it smoothly.

"When you go home, I want you to repeat that about a hundred times—every night—until I see you again for our next session. If you want to try for precision by consistently hitting inanimate objects, line up some empty cans on a fence or wall for starters."

"Will do." Man, he couldn't wait to start.

The men turned their attention to Megan who stood exactly where she'd been told to, posing the same as before. "Megan, you're doing great. Ready for me to relieve you of your remaining flowers?"

She nodded, unable to speak.

Ryder tried to focus more intently on the whip this time, but it still happened so quickly that he heard the crack of the popper and the tip of the flower had dropped from her hand quicker than a flash.

Megan giggled, but maintained her stance. Nerves of steel.

"Awesome job, baby!" Ryder said.

She grinned, but her teeth didn't let loose of the final daisy. Ryder seemed more worried than Megan did about what would happen next. Clearly, she trusted Gunnar to do no harm.

"Megan, do a quarter turn in either direction you're comfortable with." Facing toward her left, in the direction of the other stations in the dungeon, her eyes widened in surprise. Ryder glanced in the same direction to find that Marc and Angelina had stopped whatever they'd been doing to watch. They both remained silent, respectful, and serious. Ryder wondered if Gunnar might have another Dom in Marc wanting to train with the whip soon.

"Now, Megan, place your hands in a box hold behind your back," Gunnar began, "bend forward, and keep your head tilted back so that the daisy is sticking straight out toward Angelina."

Ryder wasn't sure he'd be as calm in such a predicament, but she did as instructed. Blood rushed in his ears as he waited, wanting this to be over. If anything happened—

*Crack!*

Ryder jumped, but Megan didn't seem to move an inch. How she'd learned that kind of discipline was beyond him. Pride welled up in him again.

"You can stand up straight now," Gunnar said. "It's over."

Ryder had a lot to learn, but was determined to start tonight. Marc said Angelina was intrigued now, too, so while the two women hung out a while, Gunnar gave Ryder and Marc a joint lesson.

In the hands of an expert, a whip would be formidable weapon against almost anything but a sidearm. In this day and age, it also would have the element of surprise. He looked forward to learning more. There would be a time in the not-to-distant future when the ranch would have strangers roaming around and, while they'd do their best at screening and could ban firearms, there would be some troubled people making use of their services. He'd need to protect Megan, Cassie, and others working with the program.

The daunting responsibility weighed heavily on him as the primary caretaker of the ranch and its occupants.

*God, don't let me fuck this up.*

# Ryder & Megan:
# Horsing Around in the Barn

Ryder entered the barn, leading O'Keeffe to her stall with Chance hot on his tail. The dog had been at his side all day and now headed straight for the water and food bowls at the end of the barn. He patted O'Keeffe's neck. After working with this horse, the most severely wounded of Luke's rescues, these past few months, Ryder was pleased that O'Keeffe had calmed down enough to finally let him take her into the barn at night. Not a moment too soon, as winter prepared to set in for good now in late October. The sense of accomplishment Ryder felt in being a part of the animal's transformation made him feel like a king.

Living on this ranch had transformed Ryder, too. Well, he had to credit more than the ranch for that. Having Megan as his bride had made the biggest difference of all in his life. While he still tried to avoid crowds, recently he'd ventured into Breckenridge with her a few times to have dinner at Angelina's place. Talk about crowds, but the hostess was always accommodating and gave them a quiet table in a corner near the rear exit where he could keep his back to the wall and watch both doors. Okay, progress came slowly, but he'd probably never lose that instinct to be prepared and on guard when among lots of people. It was even more acute now because he needed to protect Megan.

Of course, they'd been to Gunnar's dungeon in Breckenridge many times, too, but his house was far outside the busy tourist town. Most recently, though, he'd surprised himself and braved taking Megan into nearby Fairchance for a local celebration that brought out hundreds of local people. They'd only stayed an hour or so but had met some of their neighbors. Progress.

If Megan hadn't been beside him, it was doubtful he'd have gone to any of those places. He'd still be hiding away on a pueblo outside Albuquerque.

But Megan and this ranch had become his sanctuary. Both helped to keep him grounded. He'd be content to stay in this place for the rest of their days, as long as he had her beside him.

Megan seemed to thrive here, too. She'd joined the local arts council and would be teaching a photography class this winter. Good training for when the ranch had its first group of guests. She'd also opened a studio in Breckenridge near Angelina's restaurant and had already booked a number of weddings and other events well into next summer.

He'd worried at first about how this city girl from Chicago would acclimate to the slow-paced, sparsely populated area of Colorado they'd chosen to settle down in, but Megan said she welcomed the chance to focus on her art without a lot of distractions. She still spent more time outside the studio than in, setting up shoots in some places she'd scouted out for the more adventurous couples wanting engagement photos, or the parents of new babies looking for unusual shots. Her eye was impeccable.

After O'Keeffe was settled in, he rotated his shoulders to work out some kinks. They ached from this week's fence-mending project with Luke. It was taking him longer than expected to get used to the amount of physical labor running a ranch required.

While physically demanding, the hard work helped keep his mind away from dwelling on the past too much, which wasn't easy with the eighth anniversary of the attack his team had taken on that rooftop in Fallujah only weeks away now. Autumn had been the most difficult time of the year for him ever since.

The last few nights, he'd come in late and fallen into bed exhausted soon after supper, sorely neglecting his bride of four months. Thank goodness he and Luke had finished work early today after spending all morning and most of the afternoon mending the last of the fences. Ryder was ready to kick back awhile, and he got the impression from Luke that he wouldn't be coming off the mountain again for a couple of days.

Straddling O'Keeffe's flanks out on the range, Ryder's thoughts had drifted to baser ones a number of times. As they did again now.

*Where's that woman of mine?*

A few stalls away, he heard Megan start singing to one of the horses. Cassatt, most likely. Walking down the aisle to that door, he peeked inside, watching her currycombing her favorite mare. Megan enjoyed the challenge of this high-strung horse who displayed more spirit than Fontana.

She glanced over the black-and-white paint's back and smiled. "I should be finished here in a few minutes. Dinner's in the crockpot." She shrugged as if that was something to apologize for. "I didn't want to spend all afternoon cooped up in the house on such a gorgeous day."

"So you decided to be cooped up in the barn instead?"

"Oh, no! Cassatt and I took a nice, long ride this morning, and I have the most amazing photos of the lingering amber aspen leaves on the mountain. Then I took some shots of her and the ranch for the web site we'll be working on this winter. We've had all kinds of fun today, haven't we, Cassatt?" She patted the horse's neck. "Much more interesting than being in the house or barn—or mending fences. But you're back early, aren't you?"

"All done. Luke's already headed home to Cassie. Probably won't see him again for days."

"Finally! I have you all to myself." She giggled as she kissed him sweetly and pulled away.

Her ginger hair had been pulled into a high ponytail. Sounded like Megan might want to horse around, too, knowing they'd be alone a while. He'd been wanting to demonstrate his whip skills on her ever since Gunnar had given him the go-ahead several days ago but had been too bone tired to trust himself with a whip.

Tonight, they'd play for the first time with the four-foot single tail he'd laid on the worktable in the tack room before supper. Ryder kept some of their other favorite toys hidden in a duffel bag tucked behind the worktable in that room, too. While he knew Luke made BDSM furniture and equipment, Ryder still couldn't get a read as to whether the private man lived the lifestyle, too, or merely enjoyed using his carpentry skills in this way. Deciding it best to be cautious, concealing his and Megan's secret lifestyle seemed prudent—and many of the implements they used fit in naturally inside a horse barn's tack room.

The sound of a popper cracking would frighten the horses, but Gunnar had taught him that was just for show anyway. His mentor had let his break the sound barrier at the dungeon that time—making Megan jump—but he'd stressed the importance of precision and controlling the amount of force used over show-boating, as he called it.

Ryder had perfected his throw until he didn't make a sound. Only a swish of air as the whip raced toward his intended target. Tonight, for the first time, that would be Megan's upper back and ass.

His cock grew stiff at the thought of seeing his marks on her.

First, he needed a shower and supper. They walked hand in hand into the house, and he went to the bathroom while Megan finished preparing dinner. He sat down at the table ten minutes later with Megan serving him a hearty bowl of beef stew.

"Tastes great, baby." He reached out to tuck a strand of hair that had come loose from her ponytail behind her ear. "Thanks for making it."

"Well, you can thank Cassie for the amaranth bread. Luke

46

dropped it off at the house this morning before you two headed out."

"Will do—next time I see her." Possibly more reclusive than Ryder, Luke's wife preferred being up on her mountain, but she occasionally popped in to see Megan and visit with Chance, the mama dog she and Luke had rescued following the fire up on her mountain. Chance was a working dog and preferred to be here on the ranch. Occasionally, Cassie brought Suyana, one of Chee's littermates, along to spend time with her mama and Chee.

They finished supper quickly. Anxious to get out to the barn to play, he helped with the dishes. "Red, after we get the horses settled for the night, I want you to go to the tack room, strip everything off, and wait for me—on your knees wearing only your ankle cuffs and collar."

Her hand drifted away from the sink, the sponge dripping water onto her boots. "Yes, Sir." Her husky voice and dilating pupils conveyed her excitement. She grinned, leaning toward him to place a slow kiss on his lips. When the kiss ended, she said, "I've missed playing with you, Sir."

\*   \*   \*

Kneeling in wait on a folded horse blanket, Megan heard Ryder's boots approaching. She'd put Chance in the house with Chee so as not to upset the protective animal's mothering instincts. They'd quickly discovered that the dog wanted to come to Megan's defense whenever Ryder raised an implement to her, interrupting some fun scenes. So it was best not to let Chance be around when they played.

Megan's clit throbbed in anticipation. To ground herself, she stared ahead at the eyebolts he'd inserted into the pine plank wall, the ones he usually used to restrain her when they played here.

She smiled. *Her* pleasure, too.

Finally, his long days in the saddle were over—for a while, at least. Apparently, Luke had hurried home to Cassie, too. Newly-wed couples didn't go this long without sex. Both couples had some catching up to do.

Additional eyebolts had been placed in inconspicuous spots on the floor and walls for the rope and bungee restraints that almost always entered into their play. They grew more adventurous with each scene. She'd noticed the coiled braided leather bullwhip on the worktable the moment she came in here. Did he intend to use it on her, or was he only teasing her with it?

She'd soon find out. Following his instructions, she'd stripped out of her clothing and wore nothing but her ankle cuffs and play collar while she waited. As she had done every day since they'd moved into their new home, she'd spent part of the afternoon preparing her body for Ryder—showering, shampooing, and shaving. He liked her pubic area trimmed neatly, but not bare.

Megan melted whenever he took control of her by her short hairs, but not nearly as fast as she did when he pulled the longer ones on her head. She'd brushed the strands to the point of gleaming, letting them cascade in waves down her back, just the way he liked it—initially. If he intended to use an implement on her back, he'd ask her to put it in a ponytail.

Would he choose the braided flogger or his well-worn riding crop? So much sexual tension had built up these past few days that she would take whatever he wanted, even a little pain, knowing it would lead to intense pleasure.

The door to the tack room creaked open, ramping up her pulse.

He walked up behind her and straddled her legs with his, pulling her against his erection. "Good girl. Perfect in every way." She smiled at his praise and his excitement to be with her.

Ryder stroked the leather play collar around her neck with both hands, his fingers lightly grazing her skin. Wearing the collar helped put her more deeply into the submissive headspace for the scene.

He grabbed her hair and pulled her head back until she looked up to meet his gaze before he bent to kiss her hard. Her anticipation intensified. He broke away and ran his fingers through her hair, combing her hair and stimulating her scalp. Chills ran down her arms at the sensory overload. She loved having him play with her hair.

Draping the ends over her left breast, his hands moved to her neck and shoulders, alternately kneading and caressing. He knelt behind her, straddling her legs and placing blazing hot kisses along the path his hands had awakened moments ago. Her breathing became ragged and shallow, as she tilted her head to give him better access.

Ryder's arms slipped under hers and around her body until his hands cupped her breasts. He pinched her nipples. "We might need to clamp these for a little added stimulation later." Not that she could stand much more, but she remained silent and waited as he stood and went to the toy bag to retrieve a pair of clamps. She wondered which he'd use. They'd tried every kind, and her tolerance increased with each session, although she didn't care for clover clamps and hoped he wasn't feeling particularly sadistic today.

His fingernails stroked her bare ass, kneading the flesh. Gooseflesh broke out on her skin. *Slap!* She jumped, not expecting him to start already.

"I can't wait to warm up your ass, baby. Now, on your feet."

Ryder helped her to stand and pinched her nipples again before placing plastic clothespins on each. She hissed. These had a wicked bite at first—and she knew they'd hurt even more when he removed them.

"I love your hair down, but it might get in the way tonight."

Without question, she pulled a hair band from her wrist and quickly gathered her tresses into a ponytail before turning it into a knot on the top of her head.

"Perfect." He placed a kiss on the nape of her neck that sent a shiver down her spine.

He pulled out the suspension wrist cuffs, giving her a clue that she'd be suspended at some point in this scene, or at the very least would have her arms over her head for a long period of time. They were still novices with rigging, but Ryder had been taught a lot about safe ways to play at home—or in the barn—during his training with Gunnar these past weeks.

Megan slipped her right hand into the cuff, her fingers folding over and gripping the leather as he buckled it onto her. Not only did this type of cuff give her wrist more support, but if he needed to take her down quickly, all he needed to do was release the mechanism with one hand while supporting her body with the other and she was released in seconds. Luckily, they'd never had an issue yet, but Ryder usually saved the riskier maneuvers for when he had Gunnar's or a dungeon monitor's supervision.

Ryder encased her other wrist similarly. Her heart began beating a little faster. She loved being in restraints, especially at this moment when he took control leaving her completely at his mercy. She had no idea what the night would hold, but Ryder always made sure she was more than satisfied.

Looping the end of a bundle of suspension rope through the mechanism, he then tossed the bundle over the beam above them.

"Look at me, Red."

She met his gaze. He slowly tugged on the rope, lifting her arms incrementally higher over her head until the pull on her arms made her rise on tiptoes. He stopped immediately and let out some of the slack so she could rest her heels on the floor again.

Her body relaxed as she stared into his eyes, the now-familiar sense of freedom enveloping her as she surrendered to his control. She wouldn't have to think about anything other than experiencing what he chose to do with her body tonight. Sinfully sweet, delicious things that always left her wanting more and screaming out her release.

Ryder glanced away to secure the rope before his gaze swept over her from head to ankle cuffs. As always when he gave her that look, her stomach dropped—and his grin told her he was fully aware of his effect on her.

\*     \*     \*

Ryder smiled. The slight hitch in her breathing told him she was as turned on as he was. Beginning at her ankle cuffs, his gaze moved up quickly to the juncture of her thighs. Her mound, sprinkled with ginger curls, beckoned him to touch her, but he intended to prolong that moment for as long as he could resist.

Which might not be all that long given that he'd crashed on her three nights in a row. Taking a step toward her, he couldn't help noticing that the pins on her nipples protruded in an obscene way. He'd seen Gunnar remove wooden clothespins with his whip, but Ryder hadn't perfected that technique yet. Still, he'd equally enjoy removing them with his hands and hearing her squeals—a mixture of pain and pure delight.

He stopped in front of her and traced his finger across her lips, then slowly down her jaw, neck, and shoulders. Gooseflesh rose in the path of his finger until he reached her breast. He flicked the clothespin, and she hissed.

He grinned and walked around behind her. The curve of her ass beckoned him. He slapped her with his hand without warning. Another hiss. He longed to run his fingers between her legs to see if she was as wet as he suspected, but knew without a doubt she was.

"Let's see if we can't redden you up a little to start."

Walking over to the table, he picked up the single tail. Had she noticed it? No doubt. She was very observant. But did she know he was going to actually use it on her tonight? Probably not. It had been so long since they'd played, and she might benefit from a little warm-up with the riding crop first. Stooping down, he pulled out his toy bag.

Returning to where she stood waiting, he stroked the tip of the crop from her shoulder blade to her ass once, twice, but on the third time, he tapped her ass with the crop a few times to bring the blood flow to the surface. Looking up, he saw her hands clenching the rough jute rope in anticipation of more.

Not a problem. He delivered more light smacks. After she'd pinkened up nicely, he landed a hard slap against her.

"Ack!" She flinched away from him, but soon regained her composure and returned to place.

He knew she could take much more than this. Before allowing her to prepare herself for the next ones, he rained a dozen or so more strikes against her ass cheeks.

But the crop wasn't doing it for him today. He stopped and went back to the table to retrieve the braided single tail. Wait. He wanted to restrain her in such a way to minimize movement. Setting it back down, he came back to her, noticing the red marks on her ass. He reached out to squeeze them, intensifying the pain.

She gasped, but her panting breaths told him she loved it. He bent to whisper in her ear. "Ready for more?"

"Oh, yes, Sir!"

"Excellent. Step closer to the wall and spread your legs wider." Grabbing a spreader bar from his toy bag, he fastened it to the ankle cuffs before further inhibiting her movements by attaching chains from the D-ring in each cuff to an eyebolt in the floor. He wasn't going to do any wraparounds, so didn't need to worry about the lack of space in front of her. But he wanted optimal space for his whip to fly behind her.

Once again, he retrieved the single tail and uncurled it. Running it through his hands, he checked to be sure it was in perfect condition. The nylon popper at the end would leave little red kisses on her back almost in the shape of butterflies, which was the best he could describe them from the ones he'd applied to Gunnar's back during training. Gunnar also had applied a row of them on Ryder so he'd know what Megan was feeling, too. The marks hadn't lasted more than an hour, but each person's skin was different. He couldn't wait to see how Megan's fair skin would mark.

He just prayed the whip wouldn't tangle. That could cause a nasty sting and he didn't think Megan was into that kind of pain.

Practicing the movement his hand and arm would use a few times in the air without the whip, he decided he was ready. He stretched the whip out on the floor to judge the proper distance for where to stand. He'd need to make a mark there for future play times.

"Hold perfectly still, Red. Remember to speak your safeword, if you need to."

*     *     *

Megan braced herself for whatever would come next. He'd tired of the crop awfully soon. She waited until she heard the swish of air and something unfamiliar flicked against her right shoulder blade.

While still processing what it was, another swish and the same sensation on her left shoulder blade.

The whip! How he was delivering the feathering brush strokes with a whip she couldn't fathom, but that was definitely the sound the whip had made when Gunnar demonstrated at his dungeon. How did Ryder keep it so quiet, though? She hadn't gone with him to most of the sessions, choosing to work with her art council friends on the festival, but he'd picked up some wicked skills.

"How would you describe those two, Red?"

"Soft. Light. I know from the sound you're using a whip, but would have expected much more of a stinging sensation."

"Good. That's what I'm aiming for to start with, but I want to be sure what you're feeling on your end is what I intended. Now, I'm going to tag several places across your upper back and some other places that are safe. I'll take a photo so you can see the marks later."

She nodded.

"But I'm also going to test your endurance and how hard you want to feel the lash, so remember you're to use your safeword if I go too far."

"Yes, Sir. You know I will."

She held onto the rope above her head as she waited for the next lash.

*Swish.*

This one landed in the area between her shoulder blades, and the next several alternated ever closer to her spine. She smiled. She was going to love the whip. Delicious. Her back grew warmer as he laid another row of little butterfly kisses across her upper back.

The first blow to her butt took her by surprise, though.

"Ow!"

"Ow good or ow bad?"

She could hear the smirk in his voice. "Well, it definitely doesn't feel the same there as it did on my back."

"Different, how?"

"It stung."

"Is that a sensation you'd like to explore further, or should I return to the lighter touches?"

"Keep doing the same. I wasn't expecting it, but that makes it all the more enjoyable."

*Swish.*

She steeled herself, but the sting wasn't as sharp this time. However, the next one was similar to the first that had landed on her backside. He was probably still learning to adjust the force and precision—and her butt stuck out a little farther than her upper back.

*Swish.*

Once again, the sting. She moaned. This was going to become one of her favorite kinks. Another dozen lashes, and she started to float away.

She'd found a new bliss.

Ryder came up behind her, stroking her back, placing soft kisses on the places she knew must be reddened by the whip. He reached around her, the whip coiled in his hand, rubbing it over her abdomen and over her breasts. It caught one of the clothespins and she hissed at the tweaking of her sensitive nipple.

"I didn't want to forget about removing these before we go much further." He grasped one of the pins with one hand while his other, the whip looped over his forearm, forged a path to her pussy. "Ready?"

Probably not, but she nodded. When the pin was removed, she remained suspended literally and figuratively for a moment as she waited for the inevitable rush of blood flow back into her nipple. The second it happened, his hand began stroking the area around her clit.

"Oh, mother…of *God*, that hurts!" But his ministrations quickly shifted her focus away from the pain and to the pleasure he was delivering to her body. "Yes! So close! Please, Sir, may I come?"

"I think you've earned your first orgasm tonight for making this session so enjoyable for me."

He removed the other pin, sending her instantly over the crest as he stroked her harder and faster, pressing her body against his where his erection told her of delicious things to come later.

"Yesss!"

The orgasm rolled through her for what seemed like hours but must have been mere seconds. She laid her head against his shoulder as he continued to touch both her nipples and her clit, slowly bringing her back down.

*   *   *

Megan's release had been faster than he'd anticipated. Fuck, he enjoyed hearing her come like that. When he sensed she was close to surrendering to the endorphins, he murmured in her ear, "Would you like a few more kisses on your back?"

"Mm-hmm," she whispered almost dreamily.

He stepped back and smacked her on the ass to revive her a bit. She stood taller. "Good girl."

He resumed his place, uncoiled the whip, and gave it a couple of light flicks in the opposite direction to make sure he was ready. When the first one made contact with the upper curve of her ass, she moaned. He alternated where he let the popper land—back, ass, upper thighs—so she couldn't prepare herself. He was doing better at judging distance to different body parts. Practice made perfect. While he enjoyed hearing her cry out, he wanted it to be for something intentional and not accidental.

He landed six more lashes and noticed her hands had relaxed on the palms of the cuffs. He stopped, coiled the whip, and walked over to assess her. Dreamy smile on her face, eyes closed, body completely relaxed.

Subspace.

He'd let her float a while before taking her inside the house. After placing a kiss on her lips, he went to the table and laid the whip down. He'd clean it later. First, he wanted to take photos of the outcome of their first whip session to share with her later. He pulled his phone from the back pocket of his jeans, snapped a few shots of her complete back and ass, then some close-ups of the better-defined marks.

Ryder knelt down and removed the chains and spreader bar. Some part of her brain must still be functioning, because her legs remained apart and supporting her. He stood and placed kisses on each of the marks he'd given her. The skin felt warm to his lips where the more recent ones had been made.

*Sweet.*

He reached up and untied her suspension cuffs, and she groaned as he lowered her arms. Her eyes fluttered open, but she didn't focus on him.

Ryder wrapped her in a soft blanket he'd stashed out here earlier and scooped her into his arms.

"Oh!" She grabbed onto his neck.

"Hey, beautiful," he whispered. "How are you doing?"

Her blissful smile spoke volumes. "Anytime you want to use the whip on me, Sir, you have my permission."

"I don't need your permission, do I?"

"True."

He grinned. "But it was that good, huh?"

"Oh, yes." Her voice sounded a little mellowed out from the endorphins. Megan tucked her head against his shoulder, and he decided it was time to move this scene into the bedroom. Before he'd come out to join her in the tack room, he'd done some preparation for this part of the evening, knowing how susceptible she was to going into subspace and not wanting to have to be apart from her during this important bonding and aftercare time.

Trying to carry her and open and close doors from the barn to the house was a challenge. When things slowed down around here, he needed to convert Luke's old office—the second bedroom in the house—into a playroom. The privacy would give them more freedom to explore beyond implements and toys they could easily hide.

Ryder also wanted to install a hot tub and sauna. Man, nothing could invigorate a person faster than running naked from one to the other on a cold winter's night. He and Megan intended to live here the rest of their lives at this point unless some unforeseen circumstance changed those plans.

After pushing the bedroom door open with his foot, he crossed to the bed, already turned down for her, and laid her down gently. She opened her eyes and looked up at him, patting the other side of the double bed with a smile of invitation. In late summer, Adam had delivered the things they'd stored in his garage along with this antique cherry sleigh bed and matching dresser. He'd told them the set came from his former residence in Five Points and that he no longer needed them, but Ryder suspected he really wanted to help them save a little money on furniture. Megan's mother had also enlisted Patrick to deliver some things from her childhood home. Megan seemed to enjoy adding these and other special touches to their first home, too.

Ryder smiled down at her and removed his T-shirt before sitting on the edge of the mattress to remove his boots, jeans, and socks. She caressed his back with her foot, but he remembered he hadn't turned on the music or lit the candles yet.

"Hold that thought, baby."

He'd cued up a generic instrumental station on satellite radio, having it set to play with the flick of the remote. Soon the strains of a western string arrangement spilled from the speakers. He lit several candles waiting on the bedside table.

"Someone was busy while I was waiting for him in the barn. This is really sweet."

He didn't always do the romantic thing, but, dammit, he'd missed her. "If I'd had time to go to town, I'd have bought you fresh flowers and fine chocolates, but I'm afraid the best I could do were these." From the top of the dresser, he picked up a candy dish filled with dark chocolate chips.

She giggled. "We chocoholics aren't particular about what shape our chocolate comes in." She scooped up a handful and popped them into her mouth with a grin.

Shucking his boxers, he picked up his phone again and joined her in bed. "Even though I didn't have time to go to town, I *did* bring you flowers."

She glanced around the room, then cocked her head as she met his gaze. "You did?"

Ryder held up his smartphone and clicked on the photo app, scrolling back past the photos he'd just taken in the barn to the ones he wanted to share with her now. "I most certainly did. First, I wanted you to have these purple asters."

He showed her the photo of the yellow-centered asters he'd spotted near one of the fence posts he and Luke were working by.

"They're beautiful! Ryder!" When she met his gaze, he thought her eyes had become a little misty. "That's the sweetest, most beautiful bouquet a girl could ever receive. Knowing that you were thinking about me while out there working those long days touches me even more."

He leaned over and placed a kiss on her lips, delving inside her chocolaty mouth. He pulled away and smiled. "Baby, you're about *all* I've been thinking about out there." He lifted the phone again. "But wait, I found some others, too."

He showed her clumps of fringed sage, sorrel, and paintbrush. "That last one was down by the creek where Luke and I had lunch today while the horses drank."

Megan cleared her throat. "This is so much better than a store-bought bouquet, Ryder."

Pleased that she didn't find it too hokey, he smiled as she climbed on top of him, bent down and braced herself on her palms, and gave him a soulful kiss.

When she pulled away to sit upright, he reached up to latch onto her nipples. "Where do you think you're going, Mrs. Wilson?"

Her gaze grew smoky. "Oh, I'm not going anywhere, Mr. Wilson. I'm afraid you're stuck with me for the rest of your life."

He tugged her toward him by the nipples, and she adjusted

herself to where his hard-on pressed against her opening. He gripped her by the hips and lifted his hips to enter her, feeling the warmth of her body envelop him.

"It's good to be home, Red."

# Luke & Cassie:
# Moonlight Dreams

Luke pulled his Silverado into his spot in the lean-to next to the alpaca shed and entered the house through the mudroom. The past few days he'd come home so late that his early-riser wife was already in bed. At least Ryder had helped speed up the job or it might have taken him a solid week.

"I'm home, Cassie!"

No answer. She must be in the studio. Exiting the cabin's front entrance, he noticed the snow was falling more steadily now. He took the slippery path to the standalone studio—the only structure to survive the wildfire unscathed last summer—in double time. Thank God she hadn't lost this building. She poured herself into every piece of artwork she created, but had been forced to leave behind a number of them when she and the girls fled the flames.

He looked forward to spending more time up here alone with her once the snow piled in—both in the cabin and in this studio. There were some projects he'd been thinking about, including one that would involve Cassie. His art had been on the back burner so long, he wasn't sure he had the creativity anymore. But Cassie inspired him with her dedication to her body of work, and he wanted to share space with her in their studio during the winter months at least.

Inside the studio, he glanced over at her work area but didn't see any activity. Surely she hadn't taken a walk in the snow shower. Just when he was about to turn around and head back to the house, he heard the splash of water and walked over to the bank of windows that normally would show evergreens and distant mountain peaks. That was all blurred out as a backdrop to his beautiful bride. Sweet Pea sat half-submerged in her outdoor soaking tub, another survivor of the fire. He'd never forget the first time he'd caught her bathing in it, after the avalanche when they had been snowed in. She'd risen from the steamy water like a goddess or nymph.

She picked up the wooden bath bowl, filled it, and let its contents pour over her back. His little lady might need a bit of help tonight. Shedding his clothes before exiting the studio, he opened the sliding door. A blast of cold air assaulted him, but what pained him more was seeing her body go on alert instantly.

"Just me, darlin'." He hated that she lived in fear all the time, but at least her nightmares were few and far between now that her rapists had been brought to justice in Peru.

She relaxed almost instantly, turning to smile at him as she gave his naked body the once-over. "You should get in before you freeze something off." Her pointed look in the direction of his cock made him smile. There was a time when she'd have gladly watched his and every other man's fall off. Progress.

Cassie scooted to the far end of the oval to make room for him, and he slipped into the cozy tub for two. His sweet wife wasted no time getting onto her knees to close the gap between them, though, straddling his thighs.

"I have missed you, Luke." She kissed him, tentatively at first then more boldly. He usually let her set the pace, but enjoyed caressing her back in several long strokes before she opened her mouth to him. He reached up to hold the back of her neck tightly before deepening the kiss.

When they broke apart, both were breathing hard. "I guess you have. It sure is good to be home, Sweet Pea."

62

Rather than retreat to the other end of the tub again, she turned around and pressed her body against his as they looked out over the snowy scene. The flurry of a few minutes ago seemed to have blown over, leaving behind a winter wonderland. No getting snowed in at this rate. Maybe he'd take most of tomorrow off anyway, though. Ryder probably wanted the same time with Megan, given how hard he'd been working. They'd take what time they could to spend with their wives and not fret about anything other than taking care of the horses and alpacas.

Luke nuzzled Cassie's ear and her head lolled to the side to give him better access. Tucking her hair behind it, he let his finger trace the shell of her ear before he bent to nibble on the lobe. Her moan told him she liked that, as if he didn't know just about everything that turned her on by now. He'd spent months becoming familiar with every inch of her body.

As he trailed kisses down the slim column of her neck, his fingertip blazed a trail to her breast, circling the areola until finally closing in on her hard nipple. She stroked his thigh but didn't have access to his cock in this position. He'd remedy that in a bit.

He pushed her forward slightly to separate them so his lips could gain access to nibble the crook between her shoulder and neck. Another moan and her hand stilled, squeezing his thigh.

She was hotter than a firecracker. Maybe they ought to take a break from lovemaking for a few days every now and then to build up more tension.

*Nah.* He'd never succeed in that unless it was absolutely necessary they stay away from each other.

Luke squeezed her breast before his hand roamed over her belly toward her mound. An idea struck him, and he decided tonight would be the night he finally shaved her for the first time. He'd wanted to do so for the longest time.

"How'd you like to try something a little different tonight?"

"Hmm?"

Sounded like she was already in the zone, but he reined her in by stilling his hand. "Focus, darlin'."

But that could wait. Two of his fingers slid along the curls on her outer lips before the middle one dipped inside her honey pot. Slick. She might be ready, but he wasn't in any hurry. Pulling out, he slid along the cleft between her lips until he reached her swollen clit hood, lubricating her clit with her juices.

"Oh! *¡Sí!*"

He grinned. *Not so fast, darlin'.* The water dissipated the slick-ness and he stopped stroking her clit for fear of making her sore.

He'd slowly been introducing Cassie to subtle BDSM tech-niques ever since the night he'd bound her feet on his studio table, although he'd never broached the subject of whether she might consider herself to be submissive. The word held bad connota-tions for her. At least she enjoyed bondage in the context of art. That was enough for now. Eventually, he'd introduce her to discipline and help her to explore whether she might be interested in more.

She rocked her pubic area on his hand. "Oh! Lucas, please do not make me wait any longer!"

He grinned. She often reverted to his formal name in the throes of passion. At least she'd gotten past calling him that all the time as a way to distance herself from him.

"Sorry, but wait you will, Sweet Pea."

She lay back and sank neck deep in the water, swirling her hands nonchalantly over the surface. "All right. I will try." Sounded like she'd just lost her favorite puppy, but he enjoyed running hot and cold with her like this. Eventually, he'd allow her to come, but building up the sexual tension was half the fun for him. Patience had more than one virtue.

Suddenly, Cassie sat up and moved toward him. "While I wait, I will pleasure you."

Without hesitation, she reached out to stroke his rock-hard

cock before lowering her face toward the water's surface. To keep her from drowning, he lifted his hips. The cold air blasted his cock an instant before she took him inside her warm mouth.

*Jeezus.* He'd never grow tired of having her go down on him, and loved that she initiated the contact more often than not. She seemed to enjoy giving head a lot.

Her lips and tongue teased and tormented him until he must have reached the same fever pitch he'd brought her to moments ago. Unable to wait another minute—he'd be the first to admit he had no discipline when it came to this woman—he took her by the shoulders and lifted her lips off him.

"On your knees facing away from me. Rest your arms on the opposite edge of the tub."

Her pupils dilated as she smiled and placed herself in the position. The way the woman responded to his dominance, whether she called it submissive or not, told him all he needed to know. They could use their own labels. As long as they talked things over, came to agreement, and got what they needed from their relationship, who cared how they named things?

Getting on his knees behind her, ignoring the aches from his years of playing football, he stroked her back from shoulder to butt in long, slow movements before raking his fingertips over the globes of her butt. One day, he'd introduce the flogger, bringing her to a ruddy red. At the spur of the moment, he decided to place a light slap against one now.

"Oh!"

Her initial response emboldened him and he smacked her other butt cheek.

"What are you doing?"

"Giving in to temptation. Did you like that?"

"Yes. While it surprised me, perhaps the movement caused a tingle to course through me there."

*Oh, darlin', you are so going to enjoy your first impact play tonight.*

"If you enjoy that, we might try a little erotic spanking."

"Perhaps." The wariness in her voice told him to back off.

They both grew silent, and he decided to let it go for now. Running his finger down her butt crack, he delved inside her once more. Wetter than ever.

Ready to explode, he decided they'd played long enough out here. It was colder than a witch's tit, and he wanted to move this inside—but not until they both had their first release.

Having sworn off contraception, he didn't have to worry about a condom. *Lucky man.* He loved the feel of himself inside her silky passage as he wrapped his hands around her thighs, lifted her out of the water, and pressed his cock against her opening.

Cassie pushed back against him, eager as all get out. Slowly, playfully, he entered and pulled away, then entered her again. Each time he went another inch or so deeper. Her panting told him she was going to fly over the moon any second. With one last retreat, he plunged inside her. The grunt of pleasure he heard spurred him on. Reaching around, he fingered her clit and watched her hands white-knuckle on the rim of the tub.

"Come with me, Sweet Pea." He pumped his seed inside her as her high-pitched screams echoed down the hillside. When finished, he slumped over her. "Jeezus, that was incredible."

A few moments later, she said, "For me as well. I have missed this, Luke."

No sweeter words had ever been spoken by her to him.

\* \* \*

Cassie slipped back into the silky, scented water, and Luke pulled her against his chest. Her nipples peaked in anticipation of having his hands on her shoulders, back, legs. All right, her breasts and everywhere else, too. She had never thought she could miss a man's touch, but when it came to Luke's, she did.

They cuddled, watching new snowflakes drift to the ground as night fell. He idly played with her nipple. Or were his movements all that insignificant? He had promised more tonight. Something different.

Despite just having had an amazing orgasm, she still wanted more.

"Shall we go have dinner before we turn to prunes?"

"You made me forget all about food, woman."

He helped her stand, and she reached for a towel from the nearby warming rack Luke had installed, wrapping it around his dripping waist before retrieving one for herself. Luke worked hard physically, and she found she enjoyed pampering him when he came home, whether with food, sex, or cuddles—or all three like tonight.

Dinner was a hearty Peruvian soup he'd requested many times since her mother had made it for them for breakfast on their wedding day.

Over dinner, as Suyana played with a stuffed chew toy under the table, he shared with her the plans he and Ryder had made for finishing the bunkhouses over the winter and opening up the ranch to their first guests in late spring.

He reached out and squeezed her hand. "I have a good feeling about the plans for this ranch becoming a sanctuary for others who are lost and need to learn to dream again."

"You and Ryder are the perfect people to make it happen. I have never seen two men more driven."

"Well, don't forget you've promised to lend your hand to some art classes, too. And Megan's agreed to teach photography techniques. Between the four of us—not to mention the horses, dogs, and alpacas—I don't think we're going to give our visitors much time to sit and wallow in the circumstances that brought them to us."

"Oh, I am already gathering supplies. I think fiber arts will be the best medium, especially if they use the hair we shear from the alpacas. I have a lot to spin this winter in order to be able to supply several classes, though."

When they finished dinner, put away the leftovers, and loaded the dishwasher, Cassie remembered some news she'd forgotten to tell him. "Savannah Orlando called this morning. She heard about what you are planning to do and offered to help after the baby comes." The baby was due in late January and Savannah should be able to come out to the ranch again by late spring or early summer. "Damián said to count him in, too, if you can think of something he would be good at."

"I'd think just being there to talk with other veterans or amputees would help immensely. I'll get in touch with them when we know a little more about the structure we plan to set up. I don't expect to have many people at first, and we may even have to offer scholarships to the first ones until we know what we're doing."

"It might be best to wait before talking with them. Savannah and Damián have to go to California for her father's trial in early December. She sounded worried, and I am sure it is going to take a toll on her, even without being seven months pregnant at the time."

Cassie hoped her new friend would be able to find justice as Cassie had in Peru against the men who had raped her all those years ago. To have the rapist be one's own father... She couldn't fathom that pain, or the strength Savannah must have to go on with her life when she escaped that hell.

"Sweet Pea, it's okay." Luke wrapped his arm around her and pulled her to him. "Damián is going to make sure she's protected and grounded during her testimony."

"I know. And you would do the same for me. You even went after my rapists on our wedding night. I just hate seeing her have to face this."

"But think how good she's going to feel when she puts it

behind her and he's locked up for life. Let's hope that's the outcome, at least."

Cassie nodded. She did not know how justice was done here, but would wish for the best.

"Let's get ready for bed, Sweet Pea. Worrying about this isn't going to do any good, and I do believe we have some unfinished business."

Her worrisome thoughts evaporated with each step they took hand in hand toward the bathroom. They enjoyed a shower together, but then Luke surprised her by picking up her razor.

"How'd you feel about me shaving you?"

"I just shaved this morning." Had she not done an adequate job?

With his other hand, he cupped her mound. "No, I want to shave you *here*."

Heat rushed into her cheeks. She'd never thought about shaving *there*, although Kitty had told her she did so, and Adam loved it. Cassie supposed if she didn't like it, the hair would grow back.

She smiled. "Sounds a little kinky, but I will give it a try." With his talk of spankings and the feelings she had when he tied her feet in intricate designs, she was becoming more like Kitty than she realized.

After they dried off and opened the door to the hallway, Suyana came barreling out of the kitchen as though she'd been into something she shouldn't. Careful not to dislodge her body towel, Cassie scooped up the squirming puppy.

"What have you done, Suyana?" The puppy's doleful eyes screamed innocence, but the apple peel draped over her ear pointed the finger at her guilt.

Luke took Suyana from her arms and placed a towel and other things in her hands. "I'll go clean up the mess in the kitchen and put up the baby gates. You just take this razor and shaving cream upstairs, spread out the towel at the side of the bed, and wait. You might want to move the bed stand closer to the bed, too, so I can see what I'm doing. Don't want to nick you."

He seemed to have everything planned. Excitement coursed through her at the thought of him performing such an intimate service for her. She'd barely managed to follow all of his instructions when she heard him making his way up the stairs. Quickly, she stretched out on the bed, her legs dangling over the edge of the mattress. She tried crooking them, but her feet kept slipping off the bed. She was afraid he would cut her if she moved suddenly.

"Beautiful, Sweet Pea. Thank you for following my instructions to a tee."

"There is a problem, though."

"What's that?" He stood over her looking down, making her heart race.

"I cannot find a good position for my legs. You may have to get some rope."

The shocked expression on his face left her cringing inside for even suggesting it, realizing how it sounded in retrospect. She held out her hand and waved away the notion. "I did not mean that, of course!"

Luke's lips twitched, but at least he did not laugh at her. "You know, though, that might not be a bad idea. I wouldn't want to hurt you."

So he did not think her too forward, although he was her husband and why she would be embarrassed about anything at this point in their relationship was beyond her. However, they had never ventured this far into kinky behaviors or discussions before.

"I'll be right back."

Luke left her there a few minutes then came back carrying the soft yellow rope he'd used a few times before. Instead of simply tying her legs to the bed frame, he began by brushing the rope over her calves, knees, and thighs. Goosebumps rose on her skin in the wake of the rope.

His gaze met hers and he smiled. "Like that?"

Unable to speak, she nodded. He did not glance away, but his hand and the rope became one as he continued to stroke her legs and feet. Her sex throbbed, wanting him to touch her, but whenever he drew near, he would veer away again. She groaned, which only made him chuckle.

The man had a penchant for leaving her nearly begging for more, but she tried to maintain her composure—at least a little longer.

"I'm going to tie this rope to your thigh, just above your knee," he said as he loosened the bundle and made a loop around her leg. He slipped his fingers between the rope and her skin. "Not too tight?"

"No, Luke." It was snug, but in a comforting way. At least she wouldn't have to hold her legs open, which would grow tiresome long before he could finish shaving her.

He took the other rope and tied a similar knot on her right leg. "Now, before I go any further, I need to get a basin of water." When he went down the stairs, she picked up the loose ends of the rope and tugged on them, spreading her legs wider. What would it feel like when he restrained her to the headboard and footboard? Why was the image making her more turned on than ever?

Hearing his footsteps on the stairs, she dropped the ropes and placed her hands palms down on the towel. He scooted the lamp aside and set the basin on the bed stand. Squeezing out a washcloth from the steaming water, he placed it over her mound. "I don't know if it helps with shaving you there, but the warm steam makes for a nice, smooth shave on my face when I have it done by a barber."

"Makes sense." A giggle burst forth. "You have left me with a very disturbing image of myself in the barber's chair awaiting a most intimate shave."

He chuckled, the picture now burned on his own retinas. His cock stiffened. "While we wait, I'll set your legs at the perfect angle to be open and out of the way as I work." He picked up the rope attached to her left leg and placed his other hand under her knee to lift and position her before he tied the rope to the bed post. "How does that feel?"

"Fine."

"Tell me if there's any tingling, numbness, or pain." He tickled her foot, and she wanted to kick him, but smiled back at him instead. He soon had her right leg similarly trussed and pulled a chair from against the wall to seat himself between her out-stretched legs. He lifted the cloth, picked up the shaving cream she used on her legs and underarms, and squirted some foam into his hand. She watched, enthralled by his every move. As he spread the foam on her mound, he locked gazes with her and his slow, deliberate movements made her want to beg him to make love to her before going another step.

"I could touch you like this all night."

"I am not sure I can hold out that long. I cannot wait all night to have you join me on this bed."

He shook his head with a smile. "Patience, darlin'."

When he dipped the razor into the water, she gripped the towel and prepared for him to start.

"Breathe. I'm not going to cut you to ribbons. Put your hands above your head so you won't grab onto the hand holding the razor."

She did trust him not to hurt her, but she'd been known to nick her legs while shaving herself. How would she fare with him wielding the instrument?

What if there was a code word that would signal him if she was in trouble? "If I need you to stop, I can use my safeword—pickle."

"Absolutely. Good thinking." Again, he seemed ready to burst out laughing.

"I am serious! A cut there would be very…uncomfortable, to say the least."

"Sweet Pea, if I mar your flesh in any way, I'll let you shave me tomorrow morning."

The thought of her cutting his face made her stomach lurch. "No. I would not want to do that."

"Well, let me get started. Holler 'pickle' if I need to stop." Placing his open hand on her hip—whether to steady her or him, she was not sure—he scraped away the first hairs. His touch was gentler than she was with her shaving and she relaxed, trying not to be embarrassed. He'd certainly seen her more closely than this before, although with much less light.

Cassie closed her eyes. Luke began to whistle as he continued to work. He rinsed the razor often and wiped away the hairs. Cool air—from a draft from the heater or Luke's breath—chilled the top of her now bare mound. She didn't look down, but when she opened her eyes, she saw the stars beginning to appear in the octagonal skylight.

He rinsed out the cloth and brushed it over her before applying more shaving cream. His fingers brushed her clitoris and she glanced down to see if he'd done so intentionally, but he remained focused and more serious than ever as he worked on her.

How many women allowed their partner to perform such a task? Far from embarrassed any longer, though, she was becoming excited, thinking about the time they would spend together after. She'd probably need to shower again and maybe even go over the area once more to be sure he hadn't missed anything. Shaving outside the shower wasn't easy even on her legs.

Luke moved the razor upward from her butt to near her most sensitive place and she cringed to think what it might feel like if he slipped. She kept her hands perfectly still above her head, almost as if she'd been restrained there as well as by her feet. She found an odd sense of freedom in not interfering with what he was doing, but merely allowing him to minister to her body.

Luke began untying her leg. Time must have passed quickly or she'd zoned out. "All done. How'd I do?"

"I did not feel any pain, so you did a good job."

"Thanks. Now, let's get you back down to the shower to rinse off."

After she showered again, Luke carried her upstairs and laid her on the bed. His grin as he stretched out over her told her he had something more planned. He kissed her, teasing her mouth open and exploring slowly. He flicked his tongue against hers and she played with his as well.

He broke away, grinning again. "Grab onto the headboard and enjoy the ride, Sweet Pea."

Cassie did as he said, gripping the raised figures on the headboard he'd made for them, and watched him make his way down her body, stopping to lave and nibble at each breast and pay homage to her navel before stopping and reaching for a pillow.

"Lift your hips." He shoved the pillow under her. "Now tent your knees and spread yourself open for me."

He positioned himself between her legs. She wondered what it would feel like for him to go down on her now that she'd been shaved. The feeling of total nudity surprised her the most. Somehow, she thought she'd feel exposed now even when wearing clothes.

But knowing this would be hers and Luke's secret made it okay.

Oh, wait! What would her gynecologist say when she saw she'd shaved? Would it grow back before her next—

Luke's tongue licked along her folds and obliterated any other thought. The feel of his tongue against her bare skin made her instantly wetter. Amazing. Hooking his fingers and spreading her open, he continued licking her everywhere but the bundle of nerves screaming for attention. He buried his tongue inside her, but the sensation wasn't nearly as hot as when he moved up to the top of her hood. So close, but again he ventured in another direction. She dug her toes into the sheet, waiting for him to return once more to the top of the juncture of her lips.

When he finally spread her open further and flicked his tongue against her clitoris, she nearly exploded.

"*¡Si!*"

Again, he only teased her and then retreated. She was on the precipice, waiting for release, but had learned not to rush him or he'd only prolong her agony even more. She took slow, deep breaths as her fingers dug into the carvings to keep from grabbing his hair and forcing him to pay sole attention to the area she needed him to most of all.

When he pulled away completely, she opened her eyes to look down at him and found him smiling at her. "I love how your bare pussy feels on my tongue. Thank you for trying it."

"I like it, too. But…" She bit her lip. "Please, I cannot wait any longer."

He chuckled. "Ah, but you will for me, won't you, darlin'?"

She sighed. "Yes, Luke."

Somehow, she did hold on for at least ten more minutes as he kept bringing her to the edge, then backing off. When her panting had left her mouth dry and she didn't think she could stand another second of this torture, he plunged two fingers inside her, and his tongue stroked her clitoris until she nearly came off the mattress. Her legs clamped around his head and began shaking as he pressed another bundle of nerves deep inside her and just on the area behind her clitoris.

"Please, let me come, Luke!" She somehow didn't feel she should do so until he was ready to enter her, but couldn't wait.

"Come for me, Sweet Pea." His tongue returned to its work,

and she screamed her release seconds before Luke stretched out over her and plunged his penis deep inside her. As he held his chest off her by resting on his hands, she met his gaze, seeing the love and adoration he felt for her as he pumped in and out until she felt another orgasm building. The contact between her bare mound and the hairs on Luke's left her tingling and wanting more and soon both were coming again.

Luke nearly collapsed on her, but even in his exhaustion from making love, he kept most of his weight off her. She reached down to stroke his hair as he laid his head on her chest.

"That was incredible, Luke."

"For me, too. You never cease to amaze me. I'd never be able to come twice as soon as you did."

They lay like that a while before the cool air circulated around them and she patted his shoulder. "Our cistern might need refilling soon, but I think I need another shower." She wasn't able to get over having dried semen on her yet, but Luke didn't seem to mind because he loved playing in the shower, too, and cleaning her off after lovemaking.

Later that night, they cuddled in bed, staring up at the stars. This had become her favorite time of the day because they didn't have to talk, but just enjoyed each other's presence.

"Sweet Pea? You still awake?"

"Mm-hmm."

"When's your most fertile time in your cycle?"

His question took her off guard and she remembered back to when her last period had started, counting up the days. "Actually, this week would be good. Yesterday might have been optimal, but today is still good. Why?"

"Because something tells me we made a baby tonight. So you mark this date down on your calendar and remember to tell the doctor when you go for confirmation."

She grinned. How could he be so confident, considering that

they had had many other days of having unprotected sex without getting pregnant over the past few months? But she wasn't one to knock anyone's intuition.

Cassie hoped he was right. Nothing would give her more pleasure than to carry Luke's baby.

She only hoped she would be blessed in that way someday.

***Farewell, until we meet again in future Rescue Me Saga novels and novellas!***

Dear Reader,

I hope you enjoyed this glimpse into the lives of these two couples. Before you go on to *Roar* or whatever is next on your TBR pile, I thought I'd tell you a bit about my plans for the future of these and other characters.

At some point in the future, I'll write **Somebody's Dream**, which will be a continuation of Ryder & Megan's and Luke & Cassie's journeys in the Rescue Me Saga, including their plans for the ranch becoming a sanctuary for the wounded. It may be years before I write it, though, because first I need to do a novella about Damián and Savannah. Also before **Somebody's Dream**, I want to continue Adam's story with **Somebody's Hero** (which most likely will include updates on Marc and Angelina—unless I decide their continuing journey needs its own novella).

Now that they have come to life even more in *Roar*, I need to write about Gunnar Larson (with Heidi), Patrick Gallagher (with Maribeth Jeffrey from *Roar*), and Mistress Grant (with Liam, the man who had her kicked out of black ops). Their romances will be told inside a romantic suspense trilogy. Each couple will have their happy ending, but there will be a suspense thread carried throughout the three books. *Roar* will serve as a bridge between these two series.

But I can never predict whose story will come to me next, so please stay tuned to my newsletters! You can sign up for updates (or check to see if you're already signed up) at my web site: kallypsomasters.com.

Thanks for your ongoing support for my unique way of telling a love story!

Kally

# About the Author

Kallypso Masters is a full-time author and three-time *USA Today* Bestselling Author of the Rescue Me Saga (with more than one million copies in paperbacks and e-books). "My dad served in the Navy (World War II) and the Army's Signal Corps (Korea). His PTSD from the latter affected the rest of his life." As a result, Kally chose to write about members of a military "family" helping each other heal and cope after combat and life's intrusions. She also writes about the fallout from devastating traumas suffered by other characters in her ongoing saga. She knows that Happily Ever After takes maintenance, so her couples don't solve all their problems and disappear at "the end" of "their" novel, but will continue to work on real problems in their relationships in later books in the Saga. Therefore, the books in the Rescue Me Saga should be read in order because characters recur and continue their journeys throughout the series. However, there will be spinoff books and series in the future that will be written so that they can be read without reading the Rescue Me Saga first. This includes *Roar.*

Kally's emotional, realistic Romance novels emphasize ways of healing using unconventional methods. Her alpha males are dominant and attracted to strong women who can bring them to their knees. Kally has brought many readers to their knees, as well—having them experience the stories right alongside her characters. Readers often tell her they're on their third, sixth, or even twelfth read of the series because the layers are so deep that new information is revealed with each re-read.

Kally has been writing full-time since May 2011. She lives in rural Kentucky and has been married almost 33 years to the man who provided her own Happily Ever After. They have two adult children, one adorable grandson, and a rescued dog and cat.

Kally enjoys meeting readers. Check out the Appearances page on her web site to see if she'll be near you!

For more timely updates and a chance to win great prizes, get sneak peeks at unedited excerpts, and more, sign up for her newsletter (sent out via e-mail) (kallypsomasters.com/newsletter) and/or for text alerts (used ONLY for new releases of e-books or print books) at her Web site (KallypsoMasters.com).

To contact or interact with Kally,
go to Facebook (where almost all posts are public),
her Facebook Author page,
or Twitter (@kallypsomasters),
or her Web site (KallypsoMasters.com).

To join the secret Facebook group Rescue Me Saga Discussion Group, please send a friend request to Karla Paxton and she will open the door for you. (Please allow her a few days! She's a busy woman these days!) Must be 18 to join.

And feel free to e-mail Kally at kallypsomasters@gmail.com, or write to her at

Kallypso Masters
PO Box 1183
Richmond, KY 40476-1183

# Get your Kally Swag!

Want to own merchandise from the Rescue Me Saga, including these Ka-thunk!® T-shirts, and/or the new Princess Slut® T-shirts (coming soon) and beaded evil sticks both inspired by scenes in *Nobody's Perfect*? You've come to the right place! With each order, you also will receive a bag filled with Kally's latest swag items, including a 3-inch pin-back button that reads "I'm a Masters Brat," ink pens, bookmarks, and vintage-cover trading cards. You can even order personally sign copies of her paperbacks to be sent directly to you. Kally ships internationally. To shop, go to kallypsomasters.com/kally_swag.

# A Hot, Sexy Excerpt from
# ROAR
## by Kallypso Masters

(A standalone novel with familiar secondary characters)

Copyright © 2015-2016

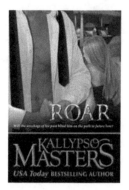

(Learn More about *Roar*)

Pamela wasn't sure what metamorphosis had occurred over dinner or why, but she sensed Kristoffer coming to some sort of peace and contentment about moving forward with their relationship. For the first time since realizing she was falling for him in a big way, she had hope that they would be able to carve out a life for themselves.

But tonight, he had planned a scene for them so she prepared herself mentally.

Roar closed the door. "Go into the bathroom and remove your clothing. Shower if you wish. I'm going to do a little setup, so please wait there until I come for you."

She grinned as she removed her jewelry and shawl, placing them on the dresser. Slipping out of her shoes, she made her way into the bathroom.

Anticipation ran high. He'd hinted at something different

tonight, not to mention that she'd been dying for another scene since leaving Sonoma. Wanting to be as fresh as possible, and hoping it would relax her a little, she hopped into the shower but used a plastic cap to keep her hair dry. No sense spending a lot of time with a dryer. She wanted to be ready when he opened that door.

Brushing out her slightly tangled hair, she then knelt on the bath mat in front of the vanity. Because he hadn't specified how he wanted her waiting, she decided to present herself in a modified kneeling position, keeping her gaze and head cast downward in submission. Instead of placing her arms and hands in a box hold behind her, she rested them palms down on her bare thighs. She straightened her back, rested her butt on her heels, and bowed her head.

*I am yours, Roar.*

A number of minutes passed with no sign of him. She could hear no sounds beyond the door, either.

*Don't clutter up your mind with worry. Focus on your breathing. In…out. Prepare yourself for…*

The door opened without a knock or warning. She kept her gaze on the tiles in front of her.

"Beautiful submission. Thank you, Sprite."

Her heart soared with pleasure at his compliment. Roar came toward her and placed his hand under her chin, tilting her head back until she stared up at him. He wore the same slacks, dress shirt, and tie. *Sexy.*

*Mine.*

Tall. Silent. Commanding. The power he exuded melted her to the core.

"Give me your left hand." She lifted and placed it in his outstretched one as he helped her to her feet. Standing naked before him, a sense of vulnerability overcame her, but he'd seen her naked before and seemed to like what he saw.

He stroked her cheek, his hand warm and unwavering. She knew where she stood with him, what was expected of her.

"Trust me?"

"Yes, Sir."

"My intention is for us to go further tonight in your mind-centering exercises, among other activities. Any parts of your body I should be aware of as being off limits?"

"No. I am yours completely."

"Any restrictions you have concerning my body?"

Was he going to permit her to touch him, pleasure him this time? "None other than my hard limits, Sir."

He stepped back, released her hand, and took a chunk of her hair, pulling her head back. She didn't fight against him. This was what she'd trained for. She wanted to please him with her entire being.

He bent to claim her lips, teasing her into responding to him with tiny nibbles and sucking on her lips. She didn't open her mouth right away. He seemed content to tease a moment then, suddenly, he invaded her mouth. When his tongue pushed between her lips, claiming her at the same moment his hand reached up to pinch her nipple for the first time, her knees buckled. Thankfully, he held her upright with his left arm around her back, or she'd have collapsed on the floor.

His tongue retreated and advanced repeatedly as his thumb and finger tormented her tender peak. Was he preparing her for…

*Don't think about anything but this moment. This kiss.*

He tugged her hair harder, opening her mouth to a deeper plundering. She tangoed playfully with his tongue, simulating her licking the sides of his penis. He groaned and gently pushed her away.

His breathing was rapid and shallow, eyes dilated. "Come with me before it gets too dark for this to be fun."

Puzzled by his words, she took his hand, and he led her out to the balcony. The sun had set forty-five minutes ago, and while private and removed from other cabins, she had no idea if anyone was on the beach below or the rocks nearby. The cool evening breeze made her nipples bunch in anticipation.

"I want your hands on the top of the railing, like so." He positioned her hands in front of her, shoulder height. Tapping her shins with his shoe, he guided her feet away from the railing until she stood bent over at the waist at a forty-five degree angle.

"See that group of trees over there?" Tilting her head back, she saw he pointed down the hillside a hundred yards away. She nodded. "Keep your focus on it until I tell you otherwise."

She'd noticed someone hiking there earlier in the day. Her naked body would be visible in the balcony lights if someone was out there, but it was too dark for her to make out any shadows moving. *Wait.* Had she just seen something move in the trees? Her face grew warm at the thought of being seen in this compromising position.

Her breasts dangled underneath her as Roar positioned himself behind her, pressing his erection against her butt as he leaned over her back. He reached around her ribs to cup her breasts. "I can see I'm going to enjoy the hell out of these." *Apparently so.*

She grinned but didn't respond. His lips nuzzled her neck, and she moaned then wondered if she was in sound restriction. He hadn't said anything about it, but she'd try not to be too vocal until certain she was in the clear.

When he released her breasts, she ached for more. "Maintain that position. I'll be right back."

Again, she began to worry whether anyone was watching her, but only found herself getting wet at the thought. Who knew she had an exhibitionist streak in her? Well, she had agreed to stand naked in front of her classmates at The Denver Academy.

*Focus on now. Inhale...exhale.*

She brought her wandering thoughts under control as she

waited and stared at the evergreen trees.

Roar returned and stood on her right side. "I've been fantasizing about placing clamps on your nipples since I saw you standing in that anatomy class."

That he'd fantasized about her during that brief incident surprised her. That he loved nipple clamps didn't. No, it thrilled her.

He pinched her nipple to make it swell before placing the first tweezer clamp on her right nipple and sliding the rubber ring up the metal to tighten it. She sucked in her breath. While tight at first, given how little she'd played in recent years, the pain quickly dissipated to leave only a dull pressure.

"How does that feel?"

"Delicious. Enough pressure to know they're there, but not painful."

"I'll see what I can do to add to your enjoyment." He slid the ring closer to the clamp's tips, and they mashed the base of her nipple until she suddenly rose on tiptoes trying to escape. "Better?"

She nodded, unsure of her voice.

"You will answer direct questions aloud, please."

"Yes, Sir." Her voice came out in a squeaky whisper. "Much tighter now."

He chuckled. "I see we're going to enjoy finding just the right clamps to command adequate respect from you in the future."

She'd heard of a number of clamps that had more bite than tweezer ones did and decided it might be a good idea to work on conditioning her nipples for that eventuality.

With most nipple clamps, the discomfort in the beginning was fleeting as the blood flow was cut off and the nipples became numb. The real pain would come later, when he removed them. After he attached the other clamp and adjusted the tension until she hissed in pain again, she realized there was a chain between them. No sooner did the thought register than he tugged on it, enough to make her breasts bob and nipples start to ache again.

He stood behind her again, wrapping his arms around her and cupping her breasts as though assessing their weight. His thumb and finger pinched her areolas and pulled them away from her body making her push out her chest to try and relieve the pain.

When he released them, he stepped away, taking his body's heat with him. The cool night air raised goose bumps on her back and arms.

"Nice. We'll let those work their magic for a while. The real fun will come later."

The swish of a flogger made her grip the railing harder, anticipating the first falls hitting her backside, but he didn't begin there. Instead, they slapped against her outer thigh. As the skin grew warmer, he switched sides and applied the tips of the flogger to her other thigh.

Hardly missing a beat, the falls of another flogger—probably a leather one—came down hard across her butt cheeks without warming her up whatsoever. "Ow!" The sting surprised her more than anything. The first flogger had been thuddy, but this new one actually hurt. She took a deep breath to center herself again and prepare for...

*Slap! Slap! Slap!*

She hissed, but didn't utter a sound otherwise. The tails of the leather one landed on her butt and the softer one, her upper thighs. Just when she thought she'd begun to predict a rhythm, he reversed them and the stings now fell on to her thighs. Holding on to the rail, she tried to maintain her focus on the trees, but it was now too dark to see them.

"Let me hear how much you're enjoying this, Sprite."

He wanted her to make noise? Would anyone in a nearby room hear the sound? Would they be aware of what was going on next door?

"Yes, Roar, Sir." The next blows were high on the backs of

her thighs, stinging more than the others. "Mmm." She loved the sting of the flogger and once again became used to the rhythm, moaning in pleasure.

Suddenly, the tails became silent and a new implement cracked across her butt. "Christ!" Unrelenting, he paddled her with whatever it was until tears streamed down her face. "Oh, God! My butt's on fire." The paddling stopped.

"What color are you?"

The sting burned even more now that he'd stopped. But she wasn't ready to stop, even though she welcomed this break. "Green."

"What number is your pain level?"

"Five to six."

"Good to know. Why don't we cool off that ass of yours a little before we continue? Let go of the railing."

She'd held on for so long, her joints refused to budge. He chuckled and helped pry her fingers free. Standing upright took an effort, too. Surely she wasn't getting past her prime to enjoy a little kink. Wouldn't that be the ultimate torture—she finally found the right Dom only to have arthritis...

"Come with me." He guided her toward the sliding-glass door, but before he walked into the hotel room, he stopped, blocking the way. "Turn around and press against the glass from shoulder blades to ass." She cocked her head, but after she followed his instruction, the cool glass became the perfect balm for her stinging butt.

"Clasp your hands over your head, arms straight."

The movement made her breasts rise as well, defying gravity for a moment. Glancing down at her tortured nipples, fearing the moment the clamps would be removed had arrived.

"Ready for me to remove these?" he asked, tugging on the chain between them to rekindle the sting in her nipples.

She clenched her fists. "I'm ready whenever you are, Sir." The sooner, the better, but conversely, she wasn't in any rush, either. And yet, with Roar, she was discovering she had a higher threshold for pain than she'd once thought.

He reached for the right one, which had been on the longest. While it had only been a few minutes, she braced herself given how angry red the tip appeared to be.

"Spread your legs wide for me." Confused by his words when her attention was held captive by the clamps, she hesitated. "Don't make me repeat myself, Sprite."

She spread them at the same instant he removed the first clamp. Focusing on moving her feet should have diverted feeling some of the pain, but... "Goddamn, that hurts!" His chuckle registered in some distant part of her brain, so she let loose a few more choice words she'd never uttered before in his presence.

Roar rubbed the offended nipple as it became swollen and much more sensitive, then he lowered his mouth to suck on it.

"Oh, yes!"

When his free hand touched the juncture of her thighs and rubbed her swollen clit, she nearly came. Apparently, he knew how close she was because he stopped touching her there and his finger slid between her folds. She hadn't realized how turned on she was until now. "So wet. I see you're enjoying yourself tonight."

"Immensely, Sir." Most likely, her wetness stemmed from the flogging and paddling a few minutes ago, but having him touching her so intimately for the first time obliterated semantics all to hell. "Please, Sir, may I come?"

"Not yet, Sprite. But soon." At least he wasn't going to make her wait too long for relief.

The weight of the dangling chain on the other clamp reminded her there was some unfinished business to be dealt with first. He removed his hand from her cleft, but instead of going directly to her nipple, he lifted his hand to his face and licked her juices off his finger, his gaze never leaving hers.

"Sweet. A taste of things to come."

She throbbed in need. Did that mean he planned to go down on her? How could he mean anything else?

*Don't anticipate. Stay in this incredible moment!*

"First, my girl needs some relief of another kind."

He reached for the other clamp and quickly removed it. *Oh, no!* Wait for it… Wait for it… The rush of pain was even worse with this one. "Christ! Oh, fuck, that hurts!" He took her aching nipple into his mouth and sucked—hard—until the pain began to recede.

Before she could fully recover, he scooped her into his arms and carried her inside the bedroom. After placing her on the bed, he closed the glass door then opened his suitcase and sorted through it.

He pulled out rope and wrist cuffs. So he had planned on playing when they left Sonoma. Everything seemed to be happening so fast and spontaneously she'd wondered, although those were the basics of any scene, and he might have merely brought them in case. How could he have known they'd wind up in Big Sur when they set out for her mother's house yesterday.

Having something other than her tender nipples to concentrate on helped, but she was letting her focus stray.

She grounded herself once more as he placed first one cuff then the other on her wrists. "I'm afraid the designers of this luxury hotel room haven't made it easy for me by providing bed posts." He glanced around, and his gaze landed on the high-back chair at the desk. Taking the rope with him, he retrieved the chair and placed the back of it against the side of the mattress. "Lie across the bed with your head near the chair."

She scooted sideways and took her place as instructed. "Move about three feet away from the chair." She adjusted herself toward the other end of the mattress. "Perfect. Now stretch your arms above you." He threaded the rope through the D-rings of the cuffs and tugged at them as he fastened her securely to the heavy oak chair.

Roar walked around the other side of the bed and stared down at her nude body. Her nipples peaked, still smarting from their earlier torture. No doubt in her mind, she was wetter than ever before. His enigmatic smile made her wonder what he was thinking—or planning.

"Bend your knees and open for me, Sprite."

She slid her feet up the mattress until her knees were tented and spread apart. His gaze went to her genitals warming the area the air-conditioned room had cooled. He'd seen the area before, but tonight was different. With her hands restrained, he wouldn't be asking her to pleasure herself—and he'd touched her earlier on the balcony promising more. The opening of her vagina spasmed.

"You're clenching in anticipation."

Was he going to reprimand her for anticipating? How could she *not*?

Instead, he grinned and knelt on the floor, leaning on his elbows on the bed to take a closer look. Dressed still in dress shirt, tie, and slacks, she almost came after having had this fantasy so many times before.

*Don't stop now, Roar. Please don't leave me hanging like this!*

He continued to stare at her. "Beautiful. So incredibly perfect."

She flushed at his praise—or perhaps it was because of his up-close-and-personal scrutiny.

His fingers spread open her lower lips, and he continued to stare.

*Please, Roar! Make it so!*

She wouldn't beg out loud, though. For him to be this close was a huge step. Just when she thought he'd release her and instruct her to masturbate, his head leaned closer, closer, until she

91

felt his breath on her clit hood. The tip of his tongue flicked against her clit. When her hips tilted upward to give him better access, he stopped and pulled back.

"I want you to concentrate on keeping your ass on the bed. Can you do that for me?"

She nodded then remembered he wanted her to speak her responses aloud. "Yes, Sir."

"Good girl." He wasted no time placing his tongue on her again, but this time avoided direct contact with her clit. His tongue laved the sides of the hood, teasing her to distraction, and then slid lower to press into her vagina. She performed Kegels on his tongue, causing him to chuckle and withdraw momentarily. But he entered her again, and it took every ounce of discipline to keep her butt on this mattress.

By not moving around, though, he was able to target where he wanted his tongue to touch her, making it that much more powerful.

All too soon, he pulled away, resting his head against her inner thigh. His breathing was rapid and shallow. Was he going to stop now? Was he remembering Tori?

While not surprising, given this was the first time he'd gone down on a woman since... Still, she didn't want him to be thinking of anyone else right now.

"Roar, Sir," she began, hoping to bring him back to her. He opened his eyes and looked at her, a crooked smile on his face. "Are you okay?" If she weren't in restraints, she'd have stroked his hair to comfort him. He nodded curtly. "You don't have to do this if—"

He cut off her words. "Don't top me, Pamela." His rebuke and reverting to her real name made her realize she'd been about to do just that. Instead, she needed to wait for him to compose himself and decide what *he* wanted to do.

"Don't move or make a sound—until you come. Understand?"

*Oh, yes!*

A weight lifted off her chest. "Yes, Sir!"

He smiled before lowering his head again, his thumbs spreading her open as his tongue continued to work her into a frenzy. He played around her clit without touching it directly until she was ready to scream in frustration. Then one long finger slid inside her.

*Don't buck!*

It was all she could do not to ride his finger, but her reward for staying still was another finger inside. He pumped them in and out, watching the motion a few times before he met her gaze.

"Come for me, Sprite."

His tongue flicked against her clit as his third finger joined the other two and pushed deep into her. Instead of pulling out, they curled around and stroked her G-spot. An involuntary spasm raised her pelvis toward him. He must have assumed she'd begun to come, but she really was close. However, he didn't slow down his tongue or fingers as the crescendo built.

"I'm going to come!"

His fingers alternated between pumping in and out and pressing against that sweet spot deep inside, while his tongue didn't let up on its assault. She began to buck up and down, simulating the sex act, as she rode to the crest.

"Oh, yes! Don't stop, Sir! Oh, my God!"

She soared over the summit and continued to revel in the incredible feeling as he slowed down his movements, but continued to touch her. When her clit became ultrasensitive, she wanted to beg him to stop, but groaned instead, hoping he'd understand how hypersensitive it was.

Her heart pounded as he pulled away, his fingers remaining inside her. Filling her. Making her want more.

Making her want what she couldn't have.

She panted, her chest heaving as she tried to take a deep breath. When she glanced down at him again, he smiled at her in triumph.

"That was absolutely incredible, Sir."

"For me as well." He withdrew his fingers and stood. Was this it? He didn't want something in return for what he'd given her? It wasn't her place to suggest that she knew what he needed or wanted, but clearly, judging by the tent in his pants, he needed relief, too.

He circled the bed again and began removing the restraints. She tried to hide her disappointment.

*Give him time.*

He'd taken a giant leap tonight. She wouldn't push him. Perhaps they'd snuggle now. Maybe he'd let her stroke him, even if he didn't want to come.

He moved the chair away and helped situate her into a sitting position facing him. He leaned closer and pressed his wet lips against hers, allowing her to taste herself on his lips. He grabbed her head with both hands and plunged his tongue inside her mouth. His kiss signaled anything but an end to this scene.

As she suspected, he took her arms and guided her to her feet.

"Undress me."

*Don't think about how far he intends to take this tonight. Just follow one instruction at a time.*

She tugged his now-loosened tie through the starched collar and tossed it on the bed. Next, she released the second button, because he'd already undone the first one at dinner. Unbuttoning his shirt from this side wasn't a challenge at all, and she smiled. When she'd undone the last one, she reached for his belt and drew the end through the loop before releasing the prong.

Slowly, she tugged on the buckle, taking one step and then two backwards until the backs of her knees hit the mattress. She met his gaze and released the belt from the pants loops, tossing it

94

on the bed with the discarded tie as she closed the gap between them again. Starting with his left arm, she removed the cuff link and moved to the right one to do the same. Taking more care with these, she walked over to the dresser and laid them beside her jade jewelry.

Pamela smiled as she returned to where he stood and hooked a thumb inside each of the flaps of his shirt, unhurriedly sliding it over his shoulders and down his arms, taking in the view of his bare chest. No undershirt. Perfection. She loved his chest, especially his pectorals.

She longed to lean forward and take one of his nips into her mouth, but hadn't been instructed to do anything but undress him yet. No topping from the bottom. This was his scene to control.

*She* was his to control, as well.

Removing the shirt, she folded and laid it on the bed before turning her attention to his pants once more. No sooner had she placed her hands on the button than he halted her with, "Shoes and socks first."

*Of course.*

He crossed to the bed and sat down. "Kneel, eyes on my feet as you remove them," he ordered. She did so, unlacing first one shoe and then the other. Slipping each off in turn, she placed them neatly at the side of the bed. Then came the socks, which she tucked inside the shoes before awaiting his next command.

But it didn't come. He sat silently. She was tempted to look up and meet his gaze, but hadn't been given permission to do so. Something told her he needed his space right now, so she remained patient, sitting back on her heels and staring at his feet. Strong veins crisscrossed the dorsal surface of his feet.

*This isn't another anatomy class, Pamela.*

He stroked her cheek, his thumb brushing over her lips. When he pressed his thumb between her lips, she accepted it inside her mouth. Should she suck on it? Simulate going down on him? Was

95

this a test to see whether she'd please him at the risk of being accused of topping? Should she wait for him to tell her exactly what he wanted her to do?

She would wait.

His thumb retreated until it almost left her mouth before he pushed it back inside. Slowly, he pressed deeper inside. It had been a long time since she'd gone down on a man. Would she be able to please him if he asked her to do so tonight?

As Roar pulled his thumb completely out of her mouth, she gave him a parting kiss. He stood and faced her, his crotch at eye level. "Now, the pants." When she reached out to steady herself on the mattress in order to stand, he added, "Remain on your knees."

She needed to listen more carefully to his explicit instructions and not anticipate what she thought he wanted her to do.

Extending her hands, she undid the button on his waistband. His erection strained against the zipper, and she longed to stroke him, but would only do what he'd told her to do. She carefully lowered the zipper, in case he went commando, but soon revealed his boxers just as he had worn the other night.

Hooking her thumbs in the waistband this time, she slowly lowered his slacks. His cock sprang free of its confines, but still remained covered by his underwear. When he lifted one foot, she slipped the pant leg off and then did the same with the other. She smoothed and folded them neatly before placing them on the mattress with the rest of his clothes.

Turning toward him again, she waited, her gaze riveted by his erection. She licked her lips, hoping he would allow her to pleasure him tonight, but oral sex might not be something he was ready for, either.

Uncertain what to do, she waited. He hadn't asked her to remove the boxers yet, so she did nothing.

Roar cleared his throat. "Take out my cock."

Smiling, without hesitation she pulled his cock out of the slit in the boxers. The plum-colored head stood erect and enticing.

"Kiss my cock."

Needing no further encouragement, she leaned in.

(Get *ROAR* Now!)

# The *Rescue Me Saga*

kallypsomasters.com/books

1. Masters at Arms & Nobody's Angel (Combined Volume)

4. Somebody's Angel

2. Nobody's Hero

5. Nobody's Lost

3. Nobody's Perfect

6. Nobody's Dream